DEADLY REUNION

JACKIE MANTHORNE

Brainspired Publishing
A Brainchild Holdings Inc.Company
Ontario, Canada

ISBN: 978-1-7387468-5-9

Library and Archives Canada / Government of Canada
Tel: 819-953-3997 or 1-866-578-7777

Chapter 1

It had all started with that wretched classified ad in the *The Globe and Mail*, thought Harriet Hubbley, better known to her friends as Harry and to her adolescent physical education students as Ms. Hubbley – or "The Hub" when it appeared she wasn't listening.

Now she was sitting in the economy section of an airplane, crammed between a businessman intent on unfurling his newspaper in her face and a chatty grandmother obsessed with conversing with anyone within hearing distance. Harry despised flying, positively hated it. She was too aware that this man-made, thin-skinned bird was soaring at such a high altitude that no one on board would survive a crash. She was also reluctant to place her destiny in the hands of people she had never met, pilots and navigators, who, at this very moment, might be arguing about whether to deviate from standing operating procedure to avoid colliding with a comet. Or they might be on the verge of peeling off the bottom of the airplane on a mountaintop, or ingesting a seagull in one of the engines, or casually discussing how many times they could circle the airport without running out of gas. What if one of them was having a bad day? Or both? It didn't bear thinking about.

To add insult to injury, Harry was certain that the pressurized atmosphere, which airline officials blithely asserted was continuously filtered, contained enough pollen, perfumes and other microscopic toxins to inflame her allergies. It was bad enough to be away from home on the July 1st Canada Day long weekend, but aching sinuses and a dripping nose made her very grumpy indeed. Not to mention the fact that she was already missing her lover, Judy.

"And I told my daughter that that was no way to bring up her children, and would you believe, she actually got mad at me?" the grey-haired grandmother in the window seat continued unabated. "Well, not actually mad, because she didn't say anything, but I could tell. A mother can always tell."

"Uh-huh," Harry mumbled as she blew her nose.

"And where are you from?" Her seatmate inquired abruptly.

"What?" Harry asked. She had been trying not to pay attention to this vexatious woman's litany of complaints about her daughter, son-in-law and grandchildren, but she already knew more than she wanted to about either underdone or burnt dinners, messy rooms, spoiled children and dusty furniture in a certain split level, three-bedroom house in the Montreal suburb of Pointe-Claire.

"I said, where are you from?"

"Montreal," Harry replied reluctantly.

"And where might you be going?" the woman asked.

"Halifax," Harry answered, although that was only partly true. The airplane was landing in Halifax, where she was going to collect the rental car she had reserved and drive one hundred kilometers along the South Shore of Nova Scotia to Spruce Bay, the tiny fishing village in which she had grown up.

"Are you visiting your family?" the woman asked, leaning closer.

"No," Harry replied, although it was not through lack of volition that she wouldn't see her family. If they had still been in Spruce Bay, she would certainly be staying with them. But, upon retirement, Harry's parents had shocked everyone by moving to a small town on the other side of Canada. True, this small town was also on the coast and just a short drive from Vancouver, but the fact that they had moved so far away had amazed many and offended some. It was acceptable for young people to leave because most of them had to relocate to find a decent job. But how dare a couple of old people do something unpredictable, especially at *their* age?

"And your husband and children?"

"I don't have any," Harry said through clenched teeth.

The woman's eyebrows lifted, and a look of incredulity passed over her face. "Oh?"

It was too much for Harry, who rashly said, "I'm a lesbian," and then immediately regretted it. She had just pulverized a mosquito with a sledgehammer, not to mention the fact that many lesbians had children.

The elderly woman flinched and moved away. Her expression shifted from affability to confusion to anger, hardening into meanness she was powerless to hide. "I see," she said ponderously as she retrieved her magazine, which she then hid behind.

Harry stifled a sigh and blew her nose again. It didn't take a genius to understand why her response to this woman had been so intemperate. She was afraid that the attitude of her seatmate was a precursor of how her high school classmates were going to treat her over the coming weekend.

Whatever had possessed her to wax nostalgic when she read *The Globe and Mail* ad searching for graduates from her final year at the Spruce Bay High School? She must not have been in her right mind when she had torn out the ad, run to her laptop and dashed off an enthusiastic email saying, in uncharacteristically gushy language, that she thought the idea of holding a class reunion was marvellous. Had she really said that she would be there with bells on?

Prudence had eventually prevailed, but not until it was too late. Her email had been sent, and her fervent hope that she had got the email address wrong was dashed when she had received an official invitation to the reunion by return email. The next day, Betty Richards, one of her classmates who had married and raised a family in Spruce Bay, had called to invite her to stay at her house. Not knowing how to refuse gracefully, Harry had accepted.

Her lover Judy smiled enigmatically when Harry had asked if she was coming. But knowing Judy as she did, the reason for the smile wasn't obscure to Harry.

"What, as your best friend?" Judy has asked, piercing Harry's Achilles' heel.

"Then kill me now and put me out of my misery," Harry begged.

"Oh, come on, Harry! You don't have to go if you don't want to," Judy had retorted. "And you know my terms."

And she did. They didn't have to discuss it – either introduce Judy as her partner of eleven years, or Judy wasn't going. But Harry hadn't been prepared to come out in Spruce Bay, even if she wouldn't be there long enough to suffer the consequences of the lingering Calvinistic morality in which residents of the costal fishing villages had been steeped generation after generation unto today. And so here she was, flying the turbulent skies alone, fated to attend her reunion by herself, knowing that she would be one of the few, if not the only, ostensibly "single" graduates in her class. She was just as married as the rest of them, maybe more than some. The injustice of it incensed her. It was mostly her own fault, though, and she was furious with herself for being too much of a coward to bring Judy as her partner, the reactions of her classmates be damned. That was why she was doing a slow boil and why she had been so intemperate with her seatmate.

That was also why she was trying not to think about what Judy was doing over the long weekend. Harry tried but failed to suppress the sick feeling in the pit of her stomach. She trusted Judy – sort of. Harry still hadn't recovered from what had happened on the vacation she and Judy had taken on Cape Cod last summer. They had both become involved with other women – Judy with an old lover, Harry with a policewoman who had been investigating the suspicious death of an elderly lesbian. She and Judy had separated temporarily, until Harry had finally – and reluctantly – agreed to accede to Judy's need for an open relationship.

And so, Judy had taken a lover.

And Harry had struggled with jealousy, insecurity, anger.

If only Judy's lover had been someone new – an unknown quantity, a stranger Harry could pretend was without personality, intellect, emotions, sexuality. Especially sexuality. If only she had been a woman Harry could avoid visualizing. Someone she could refrain from thinking of as real. Someone she could even hate from time to time, even all the time if she wanted to. Anybody but Sarah, one of Judy's closest friends, a woman Harry had known for years. A common friend, a woman Harry *liked*.

"But why would I choose to become involved with a stranger?" Judy had asked in her characteristically logical fashion during one of their interminable late-night discussions.

Harry had no answer, but that wasn't surprising – there wasn't one.

Except that she knew that it couldn't go on forever, and that scared the hell out of her.

The seatbelt sign flashed. Harry tightened hers around her hips, thankful the flight was nearly over. Once they landed, she hoped that she would be too busy to think about Judy and Sarah. She gathered her belongings – a shiny-covered paperback which she hadn't opened, an education journal she should have left at home, a blister-wrapped piece of cheese she hadn't wanted for breakfast but had saved in case hunger pains overtook her in the middle of the night – and stuffed them into her tote bag. She popped a piece of gum into her mouth and chewed with grim determination as the airplane descended into the fog.

The landing was bumpy, but no surprise there; landings at the Halifax Stanfield International Airport often were. At least she was on solid ground again, she thought thankfully, walking down the ramp into the airport. And she was liberated from her elderly seatmate, who would likely entertain and shock her relatives with the improbable tale of being trapped in her seat by a rabid lesbian for two whole hours. Never mind, Harry thought with a self-deprecatory chuckle. She would never have to see that busybody again.

She strode into the terminal, and humid, salt-tinged air filled her lungs. Home, she thought, but the dampness made her shiver, and she was glad she had packed a couple of sweatshirts and a warm jacket. She would probably never be away from the east coast long enough to forget how the Atlantic Ocean made Nova Scotian summers cooler and more humid than Montreal.

"Harriet!"

Harry turned toward the person calling her name.

"Harriet Hubbley! Is that really you?"

"Yes, it is," she replied reluctantly, staring at the middle-aged man rushing toward her.

"You haven't changed a bit," he declared, seizing her hand.

"That's what they all say," Harry replied, unable to put a name to his thin face. "But it isn't true."

"Of course not," he agreed affable. "It couldn't be. Not after thirty years."

Who *was* this man? One of her classmates? He didn't look the least bit familiar.

"I see you don't remember me," he commented, although he didn't seem disappointed.

"No, actually, I don't," Harry answered, relieved that he wasn't offended.

"I suspect you won't be the only one," he replied.

Harry disengaged her hand from the man's sweaty one and resisted the urge to wipe it on her jeans.

"I'm Wayne Williams," he said.

Wayne Williams?

"And don't look at me like that."

Oh, lord! Thirty years ago, Wayne Williams had been the heartthrob of half the girls in high school. He had possessed a full head of wavy black hair which he coated with goop – Brill Cream, most likely – and wore in an Elvis bouffant. And fortuitously for him, but likely through the luck of the genetic draw, he had sprouted at a younger age than the other boys in Harry's class. Height had been at a premium for the boys, of course. But he also had the broad chest of a titan, the narrow hips of a Greek god, and to add insult to injury, he had attained the white, evenly spaced teeth of a movie star without suffering the tinman braces so many others, including Harry, had been forced to don to achieve some approximation of a perfect smile. To Harry's disgust, girls her age had proclaimed their willingness to *die* for him. It had likely been teenage hormones speaking, but still… Harry hadn't felt the inclination, so in an ironic way, her lack of reaction to Wayne Williams had likely been one of many clues that she was different.

"Wayne!" she exclaimed weakly, reaching out to grab his hand again. "It's good to see you again!"

"Yeah, right," he said dryly.

"Come on," Harry replied embarrassed.

"Okay, I believe you," he said with a good-natured laugh. "You never were turned on to me, so you've got no reason to flatter me for old-time's sake."

It was a good thing he didn't know how little consolation that was, Harry thought ruefully, but she smiled anyway. While Wayne had been a high school god in long-sleeved shirts and hip-hugging trousers, Harry the nascent dyke had chafed in tailored blouses, tight, mid-calf skirts and bobby socks. In retrospect, she had felt like she was in drag. Her saving grace had been that other people didn't notice how uncomfortable she was.

"I wondered how many of our classmates from out of town would come," Harry remarked.

"Lots, I hope," Wayne replied. "Otherwise, it won't be a very large reunion."

"I suppose not," Harry said. "There weren't that many of us in the first place."

"Twenty-three, if I remember correctly."

"That's right," Harry answered. "Have you been back often?"

"Yes. I guess I just can't stay away," he said with a smile that took her down memory lane. She remembered how girls had chased him and how boys had chased her. Despite her inward discomfort, she had been a popular dance partner at the regular school dances, and she had dated and gone steady a couple of times. It was the thing to do, everyone did it, and yet she had felt alienated. She hadn't been able to shake the feeling that she was on the outside looking in. Yes, she had wanted to dance, and who else was there to dance with except boys? You couldn't ask a girl to dance in those days, no matter how you felt. But the chords of the inexpertly tuned piano and the uncertain but poignant wails of the tenor saxophone told her something different. She had danced with her dates and yearned for something unattainable. Despite her popularity, she had secretly lived through a singularly lonely adolescence, one specifically designed for teenage lesbians growing up in small towns during the late 1950s and early 1960s. It had been hell pretending to fend off boys because she was a "good girl" afraid of getting pregnant. No, correct that: real hell had been knowing down deep that she was being good because she wasn't tempted by what boys had to offer.

"So, how are you getting to Spruce Bay?" Wayne asked.

"I've rented a car," Harry replied, picking up her tote bag.

"Would you mind giving me a lift?" he asked." I was going to take the bus, but I'd certainly rather arrive in style."

"Not at all," Harry said, watching him retrieve his suitcase from the floor. Lord, he was slender, but it wasn't the sort of thinness that resulted from a macrobiotic diet allied with a daily regime of aerobic exercise. His body was skin and bones and lacking in muscle tone. She wondered how he had been transformed from a teenage idol into a skinny, anaemic-looking man. Then she felt guilty. She had never judged women – or men – by their appearance, and she was damned if she was going to start now, not with a classmate she hadn't seen for thirty years. *Especially* not with a classmate she hadn't seen for three decades!

"Lead on, McDuff," Wayne said lightly as Harry turned and walked down the concourse.

She looked back at him, ready to continue chatting about their high school days, but he was staring at the floor, his expression downcast.

Chapter 2

"But really, Wayne, what have you been doing all these years?" Harry asked as she buckled her seatbelt.

"Oh, this and that," he replied vaguely. "You know."

No, she didn't, and unless he stopped being so evasive, she would never learn anything about him. Why was he being so secretive? "If I remember rightly, you always wanted to be an actor," she commented, glancing at him as she drove the late-model rental car from the airport. It was a fire-engine red, mid-sized four-door sedan with power everything, but she missed Bug, her elderly dirt-beige hatchback with its stiff steering wheel, squishy brakes, balding tires, and cranky transmission.

"Oh, lord! How the dreams of one's youth come back to haunt one," Wayne exclaimed facetiously. He had put his seat back and was stretched out with his legs crossed and his eyes half-shut. "I made my pilgrimage to Toronto and found the rest of Canada's aspiring thespians had arrived before me. They were cuter than I was. Or had bigger muscles or a deeper voice or better connections. Or were more determined to make it," he continued dryly.

That last bit sounded especially true, but Harry didn't reply. There wasn't much to say to a speech like that, and anyway, she was too busy concentrating on navigating the tangle of roads leading from the airport to the highway to the South Shore to come up with appropriate words of commiseration.

"So, I sold things, tended bar, waited on tables, did a bit here and a bit there," he added. "I got by."

For nearly three decades?

"Wasn't that the turn off?"

"Yes, dammit," Harry said, glancing back at the exit sign she hadn't seen until she had driven past it.

"Well, I always wanted to see beautiful downtown Dartmouth," Wayne joked.

"Never mind." Harry took the next exit, sped across an overpass and accelerated down the ramp to the opposite side of the highway.

"Perhaps I'd better tighten my seatbelt," he joked when Harry braked none too gently as the car rounded the tight curve of the entrance ramp.

That might be a good idea," Harry admitted, easing off the brake.

"And what have you been doing with yourself?" he asked.

"Teaching."

"No kidding," he said. "Now why aren't I surprised?"

Mr. Wise Guy, Harry thought sourly.

"What subject?"

"Physical education," she replied with some reluctance. She almost always knew when someone would immediately make fun of her profession, as if physical education teacher = lesbian.

"Why, Harriet, how obvious!" he exclaimed, slapping his forehead. "Couldn't you think of a more subtle way of advertising your sexual orientation?"

Harry bit back an acrimonious reply. Wayne's reaction was precisely the reason she hated to tell people what she did for a living. And she was swiftly remembering how full of himself the adolescent Wayne had been. No one could get him to be serious about anything, not his parents or his teachers or his girlfriends. She also recalled how he had specialized in putting down other people and teasing less popular classmates and, because he rarely knew when to stop, his taunting had sometimes approached cruelty. He had been one of the worst gossips in high school, spreading rumours and creating an uncomfortable environment for students and teachers alike. So-and-so had been seen going all the way in a parked car down by the swimming hole. Or such-and-such a teacher had made a pass at one of female students, who hadn't been so quick to reject him. She was beginning to regret giving him a ride.

"Lord, I'm tired," he exclaimed, yawning. "I think I'll take a nap, if you don't mind."

"Be my guest," Harry replied, glancing at him as he closed his eyes. If she was lucky, he would sleep all the way to Spruce Bay.

The early morning fog had burned off, exposing them to the nascent warmth of the summer sun. There wasn't much traffic, but Harry drove carefully and stayed within the speed limit. Although the rental car wasn't full-sized, it was large enough to make her feel like she was driving a boat down the road.

The highway had been bulldozed through woodlands, leaving behind exposed rock, spiky field grass and thin strands of fast-growing, spindly trees. There weren't even any wildflowers. It looked rather desolate, even though it was summer. Tourists must wonder what all the fuss about the South Shore is, Harry reflected.

As she was approaching the exit to one of the towns dotting the cost, she impulsively flicked her turn signal, slowed and drove off the highway. She hadn't come all the way to Nova Scotia to spend time on a highway which had so few distinguishing characteristics that it could be in any country with a temperate climate. She would rather follow the famed Lighthouse Route along the coast, although it would take longer to reach Spruce Bay. But she wasn't in a hurry. Nothing was waiting for her in Spruce Bay except the prickly cheerfulness and the asinine rah-rah-rah of a group of adults with little in common except a high school reunion.

As she drove, Harry became increasingly disquieted that so many houses in the fishing villages looked in need of a coat of paint. There was nothing shabbier than peeling wood, especially when many of the houses had once been painted bright colours. Lobster shacks had collapsed in upon themselves or were leaning precariously to one side. The fish were gone, so there was no money. Harry had watched television interviews with fishers devastated by the loss of their livelihood and their traditional way of life. She had listened to speeches by politicians expressing concern about the depletion of the fish stocks and making promises they couldn't keep. But the vacant, dusty-windowed stores on the main streets, the barren wharfs, the boarded-up foundries, the idle fish plants, and deserted shipyards in the towns, and the absence of in-shore fishing boats in the harbours, brought home to her the tragedy of a natural resource lost, perhaps forever.

She slowed to accommodate the twists and turns of the two-lane highway, remember her father telling her long ago that the costal roads followed the old cow paths and that the cows had followed the ocean. "And anyway, roads were secondary," he had said one day when they were picking wild blueberries in a field. "An afterthought. People travelled by boat. It was faster, more direct." But roads were everywhere now. People followed where they led. When the highway was built, tourists bypassed the villages, stores went out of business, and people lost their jobs. Even the locals preferred to use the highway. It was a quicker way to get from one place to another.

Why did coming home always depress her?

"Oh, god! Not another fishing village," Wayne complained. "I didn't know you were going to get all sentimental on me and take this trip down memory lane."

"I thought you were asleep," Harry replied, annoyed with him for interrupting her melancholic thoughts.

"I'm trying," he said, closing his eyes again. "Anything's better than this."

Who else would attend the reunion, Harry wondered. Those who had remained in Spruce Bay, certainly. Most of the others were in Halifax or scattered around the province, with a smattering in other regions of Canada and one or two overseas. Would many of them have reacted like her, with knee-jerk enthusiasm followed by acute regret? What would it be like to see them again after thirty years? She had matured, but she was in essence the same person as that insecure, young and closeted lesbian who had stumbled through her teenage years while outwardly becoming a class leader. All in all, she had been lucky; she had survived, escaping the stifling life of a village where often the best you could do was to become your parents. No, she hadn't changed much. She had simply grown into herself. Or, to use other jargon, she had realized her potential.

She glanced at Wayne. He had been successful in his quest for sleep. His head was lolling, and his lips were slightly parted. Physically, he had changed tremendously. But intellectually, emotionally, had he, like her, become more himself? Had he outgrown that mean streak or had he merely become more skilful in using it?

Lord, how she hated coming back! This place stripped away the intervening years as effortlessly as the briny air removed paint from the exterior of houses and boats. Memories crowded her mind until she could think of nothing else.

"Are we there yet?" Wayne asked sleepily.

"Nearly," Harry replied.

She had just driven down the main street of Church Pond, a village less than ten kilometers from Spruce Bay. It hadn't changed a bit. A row of stores was perched on the water side of the harbour, blocking the view. The supermarket parking lot was full of cars and vans, while the church spire loomed in the distance. She had biked here often as a child – to do what, she couldn't remember. It had been somewhere to go, so she and her friends had gone. They had peddled cheerfully around sharp turns in the road and walked their bikes up hills, coasting at reckless speed down the other side. There hadn't been much traffic, which was probably why they had survived into adulthood. Once in Church Pond, they would lean their bikes against a telephone pole which stank of creosote, slip through a narrow gap between two stores and sit in the prickly witch grass to eat their sandwiches, drink warm milk and stare at the trawlers, dories and pleasure craft sailing in the harbour. Lunch consumed, they would climb back on their bikes and return to Spruce Bay. Harry wondered whether people still did things for no special reason, or whether that notion had passed the way of the dodo. Or the codfish.

Home, she thought, as she rounded a corner and the houses on the outskirts of Spruce Bay came into view. Of course, it wasn't really home – home was a cozy apartment she shared with Judy back in Montreal. But what could she call the place where she had grown up? If it was no longer home, what had it become?

"Home sweet home!" Wayne exclaimed sardonically, as if reading her mind.

This time she wasn't annoyed by his interruption; she had grown too introspective for her own good.

"Where are you staying?" Harry asked, turning to look at a pile of rubble lying in the grass by the side of the road. The old, one-room schoolhouse had fallen over. She was surprised that one of the historical societies hadn't bought and restored it. "With your parents?"

"Heaven forbid!" Wayne replied with a theatrical shudder. "They disowned me a long time ago."

"Really?"

"More or less," he said indifferently. "Anyway, I certainly didn't tell them that I was coming. We don't get along. But they might have heard about the reunion."

Harry brought the car to a halt at the stop sign on the crest of Midget's Hill. No one knew why it was called that, although it had certainly provided substance for some tantalizing – but quite politically incorrect, she now realized – stories when she was growing up. All of Spruce Bay was at her feet; her eyes followed the railway tracks, which had been abandoned some years before but still split the village physically. There had never been a right and wrong side of the tracks in Spruce Bay because the town's width was circumscribed by front and back harbours and was only eight blocks wide. On the shore of the back harbour, she could see the modern elementary and junior high school and, two blocks inland, the building that had served as the village's high school in Harry's day. It had closed two or three years after Harry had graduated and, much to the abiding disgust of the villagers, high school students had been bussed to the consolidated school outside the village ever since.

"You can drop me at the Barnacle Motel," Wayne said.

Harry turned right at Midget's Hill and drove down Mill Road, the steep incline which led to the front harbour. She and her friends had often tobogganed down Mill Road until flying saucers had become all the rage. Their metal surfaces were so slippery that they were impossible to stop. After a couple of kids had nearly been run over and another had skidded onto thin ice on the front harbour, losing his flying saucer in the frigid water but scrambling to shore just in front of the cracking ice, the village fathers – or perhaps in this instance it had been mothers – had stepped in and banned sledding on village roads.

"So, are you staying with your parents?" Wayne asked as she turned on High Street and followed it along the shore.

"My parents moved to British Columbia a couple of years ago," Harry replied.

"No kidding," he answered, looking impressed. "My parents haven't got the guts to cross the street much less the country!"

Harry laughed.

"I mean it," he said heatedly. "They haven't been to Halifax for years, and it's a major trek when they go shopping in Church Pond."

"Well, I guess they must like it here," Harry responded lightly as they passed the shipyard.

"I doubt they've ever thought about it," Wayne replied scathingly. "People like them don't. They were born here, and they'll die here. It would never occur to them to wonder whether they'd be better off somewhere else. They're not like you and me."

Taken aback by the bitterness in his voice, Harry just nodded.

"I don't know why I agreed to attend this stupid reunion," he added. "Most of our illustrious classmates are probably just a bunch of mindless idiots by now."

"Oh, I don't know," Harry objected, uncomfortable that his thought so closely mirrored her own, albeit without the accompanying insulting language. "Although I haven't seen any of them since we graduated."

"Really," Wayne said with a glance at her. "That's rather unusual. I've seen a few of them over the years."

"And?"

"And what?"

"Were they a bunch of mindless idiots?" Harry asked.

"Perhaps I was exaggerating somewhat," he said with a lopsided grin.

"Perhaps you were," Harry agreed.

"But this place is an arid wasteland of the mind," Wayne asserted. "And shit happens."

He was right, of course, but sometimes you could avoid stepping in it, Harry thought.

"Anyway, some of our old pals aren't going to be so happy to see me again," he boasted.

"What do you mean?" Harry asked as she pulled into the parking lot of the Barnacle Motel, sadly observing that the village's lone motel had fallen on hard times since she had last visited Spruce Bay. Like many of the two-storey wood houses lining the streets of the village, the motel hadn't been painted for a while. The residents of Spruce Bay were no different from the inhabitants of the other villages and towns snuggled in cozy bays and inlets along the South Shore. They prided themselves on their houses, each of which was painted a tasteful colour, often with matching trim. The first sight of blue, green, yellow and brown houses, interspersed with a few white ones, astonished tourists accustomed to the monotony of brick, stone, and concrete. But when times were bad and money was scarce, food came before paint. So did mortgage payments and property taxes. It didn't take long for salt-bathed houses to shed paint and for shabbiness to spread through the village like the flu.

"What do I mean?" Wayne replied with a crooked smile. "Wait and see," he added in a stage whisper as he opened the passenger door and pulled his suitcase from the back seat. "Just wait and see."

Harry watched him walk to the motel office and then she put the car in drive and left the gravel parking lot. Poor Wayne. He sounded unhappy as hell. Maybe he should have stayed home – although his prickly, unpredictable temperament might lend the reunion a little excitement. With that thought, Harry put Wayne Williams and his mysterious declaration from her mind and drove to Betty Richards' house.

Chapter 3

"I don't believe it," Harry muttered to herself, tossing her suitcase on one of the two single beds that took up most of the space in the tiny room. The wallpaper was flecked with toy soldiers, tanks, combat scenes. Suddenly her nose twitched, and she sneezed.

A small male child peeked around the door. He was followed by a second, slightly taller boy. Harry ignored them and searched through the closet for empty hangers. The closet was packed with children's clothes and smelled of sour milk. She found two hangers, both bent and rusty. The elder of the tow-headed boys whispered something in the other's ear, which set them both to giggling. Harry glared at them and resisted the urge to slam the door in their faces. They were only kids, and this was likely their room, although they didn't seem perturbed about having been displaced.

If she had known that she was destined to spend the holiday weekend surrounded by a cast of thousands, she would have checked into the Barnacle Motel like Wayne had. She hadn't thought about her lodgings during the reunion, which had obviously been a mistake. But how could she have known? Betty had been her most anti-social classmate. She had been the only child of taciturn, middle-aged parents, and had remained aloof throughout her school years. But when Betty had finally married, she had obviously made up for lost time by spawning enough children to field her own baseball team, or so it had seemed when Betty took Harry on a tour of the Richards' house. Harry was surprised to realize that most of the children were still little; Betty must have had the youngest when she was in her early forties. Harry wasn't sure whether she was extremely courageous, completely irresponsible or incredibly dumb. Perhaps it was a combination of all three.

"It used to be a duplex, one of the few in the village, but we tore down some walls and put in a few doors so we could use both parts," Betty had said. Her face wore an amazed look, as if she couldn't quite believe what she and her husband had wrought. There were children everywhere. They went from room to room, and when things seemed about to go from bad to worse to total anarchy, Betty absently separated feuding offspring or gently patted a wailing child on the top of its head. She had been bemused but cheerful, perhaps because she was too exhausted to lose her temper or impose rigid discipline. Harry wondered if she spent her days touring the house, extinguishing brush fires before they inflamed the whole tribe.

Children were fine in their place, which for Harry was within the confines of a school or on the playing field or skating rink. Having to live with some for a whole weekend wasn't quite the end of the world, but close. And how many of their classmates had Betty invited to stay here? Well, she had wanted to see them, hadn't she?

Harry sighed and tried to ignore her aching sinuses. She opened her suitcase and set to unpacking. She draped her blouses and jackets on one hanger and folded her jeans and dress pants on the other. That would have to do, she thought, although the closet was so stuffed with children's clothes that she didn't know where to put her hangers.

A ball of fur, which Harry swiftly identified as a fat puppy, bounced into the room and clawed its way up the tattered side of the bedspread. That would explain why her allergies were flaring up, she thought dismally as she sneezed several times in quick succession.

"That's Frisky," one of the boys volunteered.

"He sleeps with us," the other added.

Harry plucked the squatting puppy from the bed and deposited it on the floor, but not before it peed on her hand.

"Hey, gross. Ever neat!" exclaimed the elder.

"Neat" was not precisely the word Harry would have used, but she was in the company of small children, so she kept her mouth shut. They were obviously impressed with the dog's thoughtless act and Harry's dripping hand. All three of them probably wet the bed at night. She wiped her hand with a tissue, gave the boys a false smile and wondered what the mattress smelled like.

"I'm Chester," the elder announced. "And that's Bert. I'm nine. He's only seven."

"Harriet," Harry said.

"We're not supposed to call my mom's friends by their first names," Bert said.

Before Harry could think of a solution to this impasse, Betty slid into the room.

"Now, children, don't pester Miss Hubbley," Betty said automatically.

"Oh, they're not bothering me," Harry insisted gallantly as she used another tissue to blow her nose.

"My, my – I hope you're not catching a cold," Betty commented.

"It's just my allergies," Harry replied between sneezes. "I'm allergic to dogs."

"We'll just have to keep him out of the room, then," Betty said.

"I think I'll let in some air," Harry remarked. She crossed the room and unlocked the window. After a few tries, it slid up with a squeal of protest. She stuck out her head and gratefully breathed in fresh air.

"I see you've met some of my boys," Betty remarked, beaming at Harry.

"Yes, I have," Harry replied, trying not to beam back. What if it was infectious?

"Oh, I hope you left a few hangers," Betty said with a look at the closet.

Harry stared at her classmate as realization dawned: Betty intended to fill both single beds in this tiny room. "Who's sharing with me?" she asked. There would be nowhere to run and hide, no place to be alone to recover from all that glad-handing, backslapping and general all-around posturing. Not to mention lineups for the bathroom. What if she suddenly started one of her irregular but heavy premenopausal periods? It didn't bear thinking about.

"Bridget Andrews," Betty replied. "Bert, leave that alone!" she added ineffectually as her younger son began to rummage through Harry's suitcase.

"Bridget? You mean Vivi?" Harry exclaimed, her stomach sinking. Her nose itched, but she ignored it.

"Look!" Bert said, turning to his older brother. "A toy dog!"

"Put that back. It doesn't belong to you," his mother said.

"Vivi?" Harry groaned.

"I thought you'd be excited," Betty said with a smile. "I remember how much you used to like her."

Oh, gawd. "How thoughtful," Harry muttered. She should have realized that Vivi would attend the reunion. She could clearly recall the unrequited pangs of love she had felt for Vivi, and the ignoble time when she had been so desperately lusty that she had confessed her attraction and made a horribly awkward pass. How old had they been? Fifteen?

"Bert! Put that back!"

"It doesn't matter," Harry said. He couldn't damage the little toy dog which always travelled with her when her lover Judy couldn't. Or wouldn't.

"How come you brought this?" Chester asked, pulling it way from his little brother and holding it out to Harry.

It was her lucky charm, although it didn't seem to be working. Perhaps it was the salt-sea air, she thought despairingly. Could good luck rust? "That's my watchdog," she quipped.

"Jeez," Chester said, looking confused. Her turned the tiny dog over and inspected its stomach.

"Don't swear," his mother said automatically.

"You mean it might be magic?" Bert asked.

"Might be," Harry replied.

"But it's so little," Chester objected.

"Now, Harriet, don't go filling their heads with nonsense," Betty complained. "And put that back where you got it," she said to her son.

"Bert took it," Chester said swiftly.

"And you can put it back," his mother said calmly.

Chester looked at Harry, who smiled enigmatically. He grinned, placed it gently in her suitcase, and backed off. He had evidently decided not to trifle with a stuffed toy dog, which, tiny though it was, might suddenly become animated and bite him. Stranger things had been known to happen in a child's life. Hers too, Harry realized, wishing that she still believed in magic. Then she wondered whether it made any difference.

"My god!" interjected a new voice. "Such domestic bliss!"

Even after so many years, Harry recognized her voice. "Vivi," she said softly, turning to face her.

"Darlings! So good to see you," Vivi said, dropping her suitcase on the floor. "One of your offspring – the tall one with the gorgeous hair and the figure of a body builder – led me through this maze," Vivi said brightly to Betty. "Where on earth did you get such a handsome son?"

"That would be Chip," Betty said conversationally. "He's still at home because he can't find a steady job. He's my oldest."

"Of?"

"Eight," Betty replied shyly. "All boys."

"Doesn't life suck sometimes?" Vivi said sympathetically, ignoring Betty's perplexed look and turning to Harry. Vivi had been cute in her teens, but as an older woman in her early fifties, she was simply devastating. She had the face of someone who had led a complicated but interesting life, and skin which had seen a little too much sunshine. There were laugh wrinkles around her mouth and crow's feet in the corners of her eyes. She was a little on the plump side, her dark hair was flecked with silver, and her clothes were casual but obviously expensive. She was positively gorgeous!

"What a surprise," she said to Harry.

"You've got to be kidding," Harry responded as she succumbed to a belated sneeze. She had tried to hold it back without much success.

"Give me a big hug, you silly duck," Vivi responded with a laugh.

They came together, their bodies not touching, and pecked each other on the cheek. Such reticence emphasized distance rather than closeness, but Harry seemed to be the only one to notice.

"Come on, children, let's leave our visitors some time to get settled in," Betty said, shooing Chester and Bert from the room. "We're all invited to Mike and Linda Schmidt's cottage for a barbecue tonight, but if you're hungry in the meantime, there's bread and sandwich meat and sliced cheese in the fridge."

"Thanks," Harry said, pushing her suitcase to one side and sitting down beside it.

"Eight children?" Vivi whispered trenchantly as she tossed her suitcase on the bed next to Harry's. "I mean, *eight*? What were she and Dan doing? Trying to repopulate the village?"

"Don't be mean," Harry chided her.

"You haven't changed a bit," Vivi said affectionately, sitting down next to Harry.

"What are you talking about?" Harry asked, sniffing Vivi's perfume while trying not to be too apparent about it. It smelled expensive. And exquisite.

"You always were such a nice person," Vivi said.

Harry stopped sniffing. She hated being called nice because she never knew whether she was nice as in considerate and thoughtful or nice as in boring and predictable.

"Now give me a *real* hug this time," Vivi said, putting her arms around Harry.

Harry's arms encircled Vivi. She cleared her throat nervously and hoped that Vivi couldn't hear her heart thumping. When she had been madly in love with Vivi, she would have given anything to get this close to her, but that had been many years ago and as fleeting as most teenage crushes were, especially unfulfilled ones. Still, it was disconcerting feel Vivi's breath on her neck and Vivi's warm hands on her back. Reliving memories of her fantasies was like coming home in an unexpected – and truly bizarre – way.

"Where have you been all these years?" Harry asked, trying to think about something other than how swiftly she was becoming aroused.

"In Toronto, of course," Vivi replied absently.

"Why 'of course'?" Harry asked as Vivi's hands moved slowly over her back.

"Oh, I had all these grandiose ideas about what life had in store for me and I thought the big city was where I would find it," Vivi said, her hands still for a moment.

"And?" This was no longer a hug; it was an embrace. She tried to think of a way to disentangle herself without offending Vivi, but as Vivi's hands continued to explore her back, she wondered whether she wanted to.

"And what?" Vivi answered with a bitter laugh. "I fell in love and got married to a man who walked out one day and never came back, leaving me thousands of dollars in debt. Then I had a series of dead-end jobs, you know, the kind that leaves you numb at the end of the day, and you're glad because it would be too painful to think about how your life turned out."

"Yes," Harry said, although she had never felt that way.

"But I'm talking too much," Vivi said, her hands tightening.

"That's okay," Harry assured her.

"I always talk too much when I'm nervous," Vivi said.

"Nervous?"

"You never used to be so dumb," Vivi whispered.

"Vivi -"

"Shhh," Vivi urged, attempting to push her back on the bed.

Many years ago, when she much younger, Harry would have died and gone to heaven to be pushed back on a bed or the back seat of a car or even on the twiggy, bumpy and decidedly uncomfortable ground in her back yard or in the woods, or anywhere, as long as it was by Vivi. But that was then, this was now.

"No," she said firmly, pulling away despite her excitement. There were too many unanswered questions. And she was an adult, not a teenager desperate to have sex.

"You're right," Vivi said, rising swiftly from Harry's bed. "You must think I'm nuts!"

"No," Harry said unsteadily. "Honestly, you don't know how many times I wanted to do that when we were growing up."

"Don't fool yourself that I couldn't tell," Vivi answered, opening her suitcase. "Do you think there's any room left in that closet?" she asked, lifting out a couple of summer dresses.

"I put my clothes on two hangers," Harry replied, staring at the underwear, socks and T-shirts in her suitcase. "I guess the rest of my stuff can stay there." She looked at Vivi, who stared back at her. "I guess I was obvious, huh? But you didn't want anything to do with me then, so why now?"

"There must be enough stuff in that closet to dress an army of midgets," Vivi commented as she draped clothes over a wooden chair beside her bed. "It's been a long time since we were kids," she said, turning to face Harry. "People change. After my marriage broke up, I was poorer than I ever imagined anybody could be. I lost my *kids*, Harry, because I couldn't afford to look after them. Then, so much later that there almost wasn't any point to it, I met a man who had money and who wanted me. I married him about five years ago, got back in touch with my children and thought I'd live happily ever after, but, of course, nobody does. Being poor for ten years and working at a series of menial jobs took its toll. And my children were nearly grown up and didn't particularly want or need a mother. Anyway, you must find this boring," Vivi laughed self-consciously.

Harry was about to say that she wasn't bored at all when the door opened. "All shipshape?" Betty asked. "Dan just got home from work – he's getting changed now. Want to come down for a drink before we go to Mike and Linda's?"

"That would be great," Harry responded. "Right, Vivi?"

"Of course," Vivi replied with a pleasant but distant smile.

"And bring your bathing suit – Mike swears that the water off his cottage is warm enough to swim in, although I don't believe it. He always was a braggart, and he hasn't changed much. You'll see," Betty added as she left the room, closing the door behind her.

Harry opened her suitcase and took out her bathing suit and a towel. "Better take a sweatshirt, too," she commented to Vivi. "It'll probably be chilly before the end of the evening."

"Of course," Vivi said again.

Harry glanced at Vivi, but her back was turned, and she was rummaging through her suitcase, "What's the matter?"

"Oh, nothing," Vivi replied.

"Are you sure?"

"Well, if you must know, I'm not exactly looking forward to this," Vivi admitted.

"Is anyone?"

"Touché," Vivi said with a laugh. "Well, I suppose we'd better go down and get reacquainted with Dan. What does he do? Fish? Lord, I never thought we'd end up working at such ordinary jobs. But I suppose that's youth for you. You think you're going to set the world on fire and then you realize that the world barely knows you exist. And we've all got to make a living, right?"

"Right," Harry said lightly, feeling slightly depressed. First Wayne, now Vivi. She hoped that the weekend wasn't going to consist of a series of discussions with former classmates who were dissatisfied, discontent with their lives, and looking for change. And why had Vivi come on to her like that? They weren't perfect strangers, but they hadn't seen each other for so many years that what had happened had shocked her.

"Come on, it's time to face the music," Vivi said, tossing her bathing suit over her shoulder.

Harry wrapped her bathing suit in a sweatshirt and followed Vivi from the room.

"I just hope Dan hasn't turned into a total slob, you know, knocking back beer and sauerkraut like there's no tomorrow," Vivi commented as she led the way along the ill-lit and toy-cluttered hall to the stairs.

"What?" Harry sputtered.

"You know," Vivi said.

No, she didn't, although she had a pretty good idea, which didn't make her any fonder of Vivi. But Harry kept her mouth shut and trailed after her.

The offer of a drink was beginning to sound better and better.

Chapter 4

Harry sat in the back of Betty and Dan's Datsun with Vivi and let Betty's continuous patter wash over her. She was telling a story about one of her kids, one Harry's hadn't met yet. Harry stared out the window at the greenery of early summer. The grass and shrubs and leaves on the trees were young and fresh. Later, in a couple of months, this new growth would turn a darker shade in preparation for fall and eventual dissolution.

Dan said something which made Betty and Vivi laugh, and Harry looked up.

"Isn't that right, Harriet?" Dan said, turning briefly to look at her.

"I suppose so," Harry replied, which made them laugh all the more. "Sorry, I was looking out the window and thinking about the old days," Harry lied, patting Dan on the back. Contrary to Vivi's disparaging prediction, Dan had become a wiry, quiet, tired-looking man who looked ten years older than he was and who drank scotch on the rocks rather than beer. He went fishing when there was work and worried about supporting his large family when there wasn't.

"It's funny; we went through school together, so we thought we knew each other. But we don't, do we?" Betty commented.

"Hell, no," Dan replied emphatically. "I mean, look at Mike."

"What about Mike?" Harry asked.

"One day he got religion and put one of those collars on," Dan said, shaking his head. "Who would have believed it? He was a much of a hell-raiser in school as Wayne Williams."

"Him!" Vivi said with an involuntary shudder.

"Why, have you seen him?" Betty asked. "I heard he might be coming."

"No, I haven't," Vivi replied swiftly.

"Well, I have," Harry announced. "I gave him a lift from the airport."

"What a drag," Vivi said plaintively.

"Did you never run into him in Toronto?" Harry asked.

"Of course, not," Vivi responded testily. "Never. It's a big city."

Harry hadn't thought that it was an unreasonable question, and Vivi's curt denial led her to believe that Vivi and Wayne had indeed become reacquainted in Toronto. But why would she deny it in such an emphatic manner? On the other hand, if she hadn't seen him for decades, why would she react so strongly when his name was mentioned?

"You know, I can't imagine Linda marrying a minister," Vivi commented.

Linda had been the first of them to lose her virginity, or so rumour had it – a rumour which Linda had never exactly denied. They had been in Grade 10, Harry remembered, and it had been quite a scandal. None of them had been able to look her in the eyes. Her tampering in things adult made her different. She had been ostracized, but that hadn't deterred Linda; she had a seemingly voracious appetite for men and sex, although these things hadn't been talked about then. And they still weren't, at least not with perfect frankness. The mothers had been scandalized, the fathers titillated, although not one of them would have admitted it on pain of death. But these days, few people were scandalized by adolescent sex, teenage pregnancy or unmarried couples living together.

"Did they get married before or after Mike decided to enter the ministry?" Harry asked astutely.

"Oh, they had already been married for a couple of years when he decided to go to Halifax to study at the divinity school," Betty replied.

"Then it was rather a huge shock for Linda," Harry said.

"So I understand," Betty answered. "I heard she was ready to leave him, although she never did."

"Did she stop fooling around?" Vivi asked.

"What a question," Dan said with an uncomfortable chuckle.

Vivi rolled her eyes at Harry, who just smiled.

"I think she must have," Betty replied. "I haven't heard anything for ages."

"Or maybe she just got better at keeping the lid on," Vivi suggested.

"That's pretty hard in a village as small as this," Betty said with a laugh. "Not impossible, but difficult. And Linda does work full-time as well as being a minister's wife, so all in all, she has her hands full."

"Here we are," Dan announced. He drove off the gravel road to park. There was only one other vehicle there, a black jeep. "That's Mike and Linda's," Dan said, pointing at the jeep as he got out of the Datsun.

"Don't tell me we're the first ones here," Vivi said.

"Looks like it," Harry said, stretching.

"I *despise* being early," Vivi complained.

"Never mind," Harry said. "It'll give us time to get reacquainted with Mike and Linda."

"What a thrill," Vivi muttered, walking down the grassy incline which led to the cottage.

"Look, if you feel like that, why did you bother to come in the first place?" Harry asked, following closely behind.

"It sounded like a good idea at the time," Vivi admitted. "But only for a very short time," she added with a wry laugh. "I should have stayed at home where I belong, but by the time I realized it, I had booked my flight and promised to stay with Betty. Not that she would have missed me, but I didn't realize that until I got here."

Vivi's misgivings about the reunion were so like her own that Harry immediately stopped being annoyed. "I know," Harry conceded. "I feel the same way."

"Oh, lord," Vivi laughed. "What a bunch of idiots we are!"

"But this is wonderful!" Harry exclaimed, stopping to admire the view. The Schmidts had built their cottage on a gentle slope which led to a beach sheltered by a copse of mature trees. The cottage had been constructed with wood and the roof finished with brown shingles so that the entire structure blended into the environment. The beach was wide and sandy, and a sleek speedboat was tethered off a sturdy dock.

"It is rather pleasant, isn't it?" Betty said. "I always thought it was one of the nicest cottages around."

It looked as perfect as a scene on a postcard, Harry thought.

The front door opened and a voluptuous woman with bleached blonde hair dressed in short-shorts and a tight, low-cut tank top rushed toward them from the cottage. "I told Mike you'd both look like a million dollars, and I was right!"

"You've got to be kidding," Vivi retorted, but Harry could see that she was pleased.

"I never joke about things like that," Linda replied, and for some reason which escaped Harry, this sent both Linda and Vivi into gales of laughter.

"And Harriet scarcely looks a year older than when we graduated," Vivi added once she had stopped laughing.

"Tell us your secret, Harriet," Betty urged.

Harry privately thought that Linda was the one who hadn't changed much, but perhaps that was because she had already looked old at eighteen. Since then, an additional hardness had been added to her features, as if her disgust in the deal the world had dealt her had increased without any awareness of her role in shuffling the cards.

"Yes, let us in on the location of the fountain of youth," Vivi joked.

"It must be due to the scarcity of men in her life," came a male voice from behind them.

"Why, if it isn't Wayne Williams," Linda gushed. "I didn't hear you arrive."

"Oh, I just slipped in with the tide," he quipped with a knowing smile.

"Darling, so good to see you," Vivi said, her barely civil voice belying her words.

"Yes, it's been a long time, hasn't it?" Wayne said as he gave Vivi a cursory kiss on the cheek. "We'll have to rectify that when we get home, won't we?"

"Of course we will," Vivi replied, her voice dripping with insincerity.

"Wayne," Harry said coolly, extending her hand.

"Harriet," Wayne responded, his lips curling as he shook it. "Harriet was kind enough to give me a lift from the airport this afternoon," he added as he playfully slapped Dan on the back and kissed Betty.

"Then you two have already had a chance to catch up," Linda remarked.

"You'd better believe it. There are no secrets between us, not anymore," Wayne claimed, giving Harry an amused look which she could have wiped off his miserable face with the back of her hand. It was amazing how swiftly she could come to dislike someone she hadn't thought of in thirty years.

"But I'm forgetting my manners," Linda exclaimed. "Come in for drinks."

"Where's Mike?" Vivi asked as they trailed after her like lemmings, following her up the walk and into the cottage. The high, cathedral ceilings glowed with recessed lighting and the rich hardwood floors gleamed.

"He was delayed in the village," Linda replied. "A sudden death."

"A preacher's work is never done," Wayne quipped.

"Wayne," Betty scolded.

"You can always tell a mother," Wayne joked. "Now where's that drink?"

"He's still as impossible as ever," Linda said affectionately as Wayne crossed the room to the bar and poured himself a double scotch.

"He's a first-class jerk," Vivi said, "But I want a drink, too."

Harry watched Vivi as she drew alongside Wayne, who listened for a moment, nodded, and then made her a rum and Coke. He handed it to her with a sardonic smile, said something, and then blocked Vivi's hand as it rose to slap him.

"I wonder what *that* was all about," Betty said.

"I don't really want to know," Dan responded. "Although I could use a stiff drink right about now."

"You and me both," Harry added. What was with Vivi, anyway? Why was she so angry with Wayne when she claimed not to have seen him for thirty years?

"Nice place," Vivi said to Linda as she returned from the bar. Her facial colour was heightened but that was the only outward sign of the scene which had just unfolded before their eyes.

"Thanks! We designed it ourselves," Linda preened.

"I love the wood," Harry said, watching Wayne top up his scotch and walk through the patio doors. "Where do those doors lead?"

"To the beach," Linda responded.

Harry went to the bar, prepared herself a rum and Coke and went outside. It was dusk. The sun was setting behind a wooded island not far offshore. Rays of sunlight cut through the treetops and painted ragged shadows on the grey-blue water.

"Who's that?" asked a man moving out from behind a tree.

"Harriet Hubbley," she replied.

"Harriet," he said, his hand outstretched. He was a tall man dressed in a tan suit, and his voice was deep. She didn't recognize him at first, but then the white clerical collar gave him away.

"Mike," she said, taking his hand.

"No fair," he laughed heartily. "This darn flea collar is a dead give-away!"

"Not really," Harry protested.

"Don't try to deceive me," he said with mock seriousness.

"Sorry, pastor," she said meekly.

"Seriously, though, it's good to see you," he said, slipping his hands into his pockets.

"You too," Harry said, gazing at him in the dwindling light. He looked tired; but then, Linda had said he was attending to a family that had suffered the sudden death of a loved one. "You should go make yourself a drink."

"And get out of this garb," he added, fingering his collar. "Who's here?"

"Betty and Dan brought Vivi and me," she replied. "And Wayne Williams is here."

Mike stiffened ever so slightly that Harry thought she had imagined it. Did everyone dislike Wayne Williams?

"A drink and then I'll start the barbecue," Mike sighed.

"If you need some help, I'm experienced," Harry offered. "With steaks, I mean," she added with a laugh.

"I'll remember that," he said with a smile.

She sipped her drink and watched as he walked away.

"Harriet? Is that really you?"

"The one and only," she replied with a glance at her near-empty glass. She had downed that rum and Coke too swiftly for her own good.

"I didn't think you'd come," said a plump woman in plaid shorts which were much too tight. Her face was pasty, her hair lank, her face heavy. She was accompanied by a man who was just as plump and pale and who was wearing black track pants and a golf shirt. "I figured all you big city folk would think this was beneath you, but I guess I was wrong, wasn't I?"

"Yes, you were," Harry answered, relieved that the plump woman couldn't read her mind.

"You don't know me, do you?"

"Ah – no," Harry admitted.

"Or him," she added, gesturing to the man standing behind him.

"No, I don't."

"I'm Margaret Ross," she said with a certain stiff, small-town dignity which might have been endearing but wasn't, possibly because Harry recognized it and discounted its manipulative function.

"Margaret? Margaret Ross?" Harry said, trying not to sound astonished.

"And this is Eddie Foster," Margaret told Harry.

Well, there were bound to be people who had changed beyond all recognition over thirty years, Harry reasoned. And two of them were standing right in front of her. The adolescent Margaret Ross had been thin and vivacious, not round and earnest. And Eddie Foster had been a shy, skinny boy who matured late and sat in the back row hoping to be ignored, not this red-faced, rotund man in track pants.

"Margaret and Eddie," Harry said. "I am so glad to see you!"

Eddie smiled for a second and then looked uncertain.

"I mean it," Harry assured them, and then realized that she did. Perhaps she had grown tired of complicated city types, although they were not unlike herself, she admitted reluctantly. "It's such a beautiful evening, isn't it? Let's walk down to the water."

"I'll just get us something to drink," Eddie offered. "What will you have?"

"Rum and Coke," she replied, handing him her glass. "Light on the rum, heavy on the Coke."

"We'll be over there," Margaret told him, pointing in the direction of the beach.

"Don't worry, I'll find you," he said with a special smile.

They cared about each other, Harry realized, and she felt a sentimental gladness which might have surprised her if she hadn't been in Spruce Bay.

"Let's be off," Margaret said importantly, grasping Harry by the arm.

"Certainly," Harry agreed, feeling herself being propelled toward the sand.

"So, you never married," Margaret commented as they reached the water's edge.

It was the question Harry had been waiting for, but now that it had come, she found that she was annoyed. Fending off Margaret's inquisitiveness was going to distract her from the beauty of the sunset, the velvet ocean and the swiftly darkening sky, which was becoming alive with stars. "No," Harry said finally. "But neither did you."

"Not for the same reason you didn't," Margaret said, giving Harry a look.

Harry had no response to that comment. How did Margaret know? Was it her short hair the way she dressed? Walked? Breathed? Give it up, she thought. Somebody probably told her. Wayne. Or Vivi. Or maybe everyone always knew. There was a thought; all that wasted time and effort hanging out in the closet.

"I've brought out drinks," Eddie said quietly.

Harry took her rum and Coke from Eddie, wondering whether she could beat a hasty retreat and return to the cottage.

"They're all getting drunk back there," Eddie said. "It's because Mike had a funeral or something and got home late, so there won't be anything to eat for hours."

"Well, drink up," Margaret tittered.

Harry watched the two of them empty their glasses.

"Come on, Harry, keep up," Eddie burped.

Harry smiled and took a sip.

"Party pooper!" he said.

Harry smiled and raised her glass but didn't drink. She had already had enough this evening.

"Margaret, let's have another," Eddie said with a grin, pulling a mickey of rum from his back pocket and splashing a couple inches of rum in his and then Margaret's glass.

"Enjoy, you two!" she said. "I have to run – I promised Mike that I'd help with the barbecue."

"Oh – we shouldn't keep you then," Eddie said.

"We'll have plenty of time to talk over the weekend," Margaret said with a lopsided smile.

"I'm sure we will," Harry agreed.

Chapter 5

Harry had begun to walk toward the house before she realized how dark it was. Night had arrived while she had been talking with Margaret and Eddie on the beach, but she hadn't noticed because the last rays of the sun had been reflecting on the water, surrounding them with millions of wet, sparkling fireflies. She slowly negotiated her way between the trees, brushing the branches away from her face. She was as noisy as she imagined a wildebeest would be rampaging through the jungle. Or did wildebeests roam only on the plains? For a teacher, her knowledge of certain things was especially deficient.

There was a noise nearby and she stopped, her hand tightening on the branch of a tree. She could hear voices coming from the beach behind her and from the brightly lit cottage in front of her, but the sound she had heard in the darkness had not been a voice.

"Who's there?" she said.

There was no reply.

"I know you're there," she said with less certainty.

The silence was deafening.

She was suddenly afraid. She must have been away from the countryside for too long, she thought; otherwise, a little unidentifiable noise wouldn't startle her. She released the branch and forced herself to move toward the house. Whatever – or whoever – had startled her was either gone or hiding.

"Darling, where have you been?" Vivi asked plaintively as Harry slid through the open patio doors. "We're all quite spiffed and simply perishing for food, which Mike promised would be immediately forthcoming what seems like hours ago."

"Have another drink," Linda urged.

"I've already got one," Harry said, holding out her glass. "Although I'd appreciate some Coke a couple of ice cubes."

"Coke and ice coming up," Linda promised, wandering away.

From the vacant look in Linda's eyes, Harry knew she wouldn't see either her hostess or the fixings for her drink any time soon. It didn't matter, she decided, taking a sip of warm rum and coke.

"This is disgusting," Vivi confided in a loud whisper. "Simply disgusting!"

'Shhh!" Harry admonished.

"But I haven't had anything to eat since yesterday," Vivi said mournfully.

Vivi must have skipped breakfast, and neither of them had bothered with lunch, so no wonder she was drunk. Harry took the glass from Vivi's hand and led her to the wicker sofa. "Sit down and I'll find you something to eat."

"There will never again be anything to eat," Vivi announced.

"Well, I'll bring you so coffee, then," Harry promised with a grin. "Now, stay there and don't drink anything else."

Betty and Dan were in the kitchen with Linda, the three of them talking in urgent but low voices. Harry cleared her throat. "I'm afraid Vivi is in need of something non-alcoholic and preferably some solid food to eat," she said.

"But we don't know what to do with Teresa," Linda said.

"Teresa? Teresa Middleton, you mean?" Harry asked. "Is she here?"

"Yes," Betty replied.

"Unfortunately," Linda added.

Harry recalled the cherubic girl who had excelled in domestic science and sports and pondered why her presence at the barbecue was an issue. "What's the problem?"

"The problem is that she's crazy," Linda said emphatically.

"Now Linda, it's not that at all," Dan protested. "She's just different."

"I don't understand," Harry said slowly. "Is she mentally ill?"

"Yes," Linda replied.

"No," asserted Dan.

"She's been born again, that's all," Betty interjected.

That's all? That was more than enough, Harry thought.

"She's out there with Mike, hanging around the barbeque and driving him crazy because she won't step into this den of iniquity with its cigarettes and booze," Linda said bitterly. "And since he's a minister, she holds him responsible for all this sacrilegious behavior."

"Who smokes?" Harry asked, sniffing. Alcohol fumes and the scent of perfume wafted through the air, but there wasn't a trace of cigarette smoke. They had all puffed away in high school, daring each other to inhale, coughing and choking and in some cases turning green in the face and throwing up, but most of them hadn't persisted. Those who had were quitting or at least trying to.

"Wayne," Linda replied. "And me. But not much."

I should have known, Harry thought.

"I haven't seen Wayne for a while, actually," Betty said absently. "I wonder where he is?"

"Who cares?" Linda responded. "What I need to know is what we're going to do with Teresa. We never thought she'd come, and now that she has, she's a pain in the butt."

"I think we should pretend there's nothing wrong," Harry said blithely.

"What?" Betty said, startled.

"Yes, ignore it," Harry continued. "After all, no one said that the reunion was going to be alcohol or smoke free, did they?"

"Or sin free," Linda added fatuously.

"Don't get cute," Harry chuckled.

"Well, no, and Teresa shouldn't have expected it to be," Dan replied.

"She's got no right to make us feel guilty," Betty agreed.

"Try telling that to Mike," Linda said. "There are some parishioners who think their minister shouldn't even have alcohol in his house except for the rubbing kind."

"And Teresa is one of them," Harry surmised.

"No, she doesn't go to our church," Linda answered. "That's what makes it so galling. But what can we do? If it was up to me, I'd tell her to stuff it, but as a minister's wife, I can't say something like that."

"Teresa never gave me the time of day even before she got religion," Dan told them. "She used to look through me like I wasn't there. Maybe it was something I did in grade three. I seem to remember looking up her skirt. Not that there was much to see…"

"Oh, come off it," Linda scoffed.

"No, I mean it," Dan said with complete equanimity. "Don't you remember me doing the same thing to you?"

"Of course not!" Linda retorted.

"Never mind, then," Dan said with a grin. "You women can decide how to handle this. I'm going to get another scotch."

"I promised Vivi I'd bring her some coffee," Harry said, looking around the kitchen counter for a coffee pot but not finding one. "She's had a little too much to drink."

"Harriet, didn't you and Teresa get along?" Linda asked. "Weren't you neighbors for a time, until her parents built that house on the outskirts of town?"

"Now wait just a minute," Harry protested. "You don't know what you're asking me to do."

"Oh, believe me, I do," Linda said, picking up her glass and taking a sip. "I'll tell you what. If you run interference with Teresa so Mike can get those steaks cooked, I'll make a pot of coffee for Vivi. Either that, or Betty can do it."

"Actually, I'd better go make sure Dan doesn't have another drink or there'll be no one fit to drive us home tonight," Betty said.

Oh great, Harry thought as she watched Betty leave the kitchen. How could they delegate a lesbian to confront a born-again Christian? It was like sending Daniel into the lion's den. She snorted at her unintentional pun and took a sip of her drink. "Never mind," she muttered. "It's not the first time I've been on a fool's errand." She opened the fridge, found a bottle of Coke, poured some into her glass of rum, and then walked out to the patio.

"Well, hello there," Mike said with a wave of a barbeque fork. He sounded desperate.

"Why didn't you call me? I told you I'd help," Harry reminded him. "Hi, Teresa. Linda told me you were here. It's great to see you again."

Teresa started at her but said nothing. Being born again didn't mean having to be impolite, Harry thought, feeling irritated. She was instinctively predisposed to distrust religious fundamentalists, but she had told Linda she would try. "How are you doing?"

"Fine," Teresa said curtly just before she turned away.

"We're not quite ready to eat," Mike told Harry. He glanced at Teresa to make sure she wasn't looking, and then shrugged at Harry.

Harry shrugged back. "Smells good," she said, glancing at the thick slabs of meat sizzling on the grill. "What can I do?"

"Help me get the potatoes out," he suggested, handing her the fork.

Harry took the fork from him and put her drink down on the closest patio table.

"The devil's brew!" Teresa shouted.

"What the hell?" Harry exclaimed, rooted to the spot as Teresa's outstretched hand swept her glass from the table. It broke into a thousand pieces on the tiled patio.

"Mike! Harriet!" Linda cried hysterically, running out the patio door from the kitchen.

"It's okay, she just broke a glass," Harry said reassuringly although she felt that she needed reassurance herself.

"What? Who said anything about a glass? It's Vivi!" Linda said breathlessly.

"What happened to Vivi?" Harry asked, immediately forgetting about Teresa's reaction to her rum and Coke. "Is she hurt?"

"No, she's not," Linda said.

"What are you talking about, then?" Mike asked impatiently, taking the fork from Harry's hand and spearing a steak which was dripping so much fat that the coals were flaming.

"Wayne's dead," Linda said, wringing her hands together.

"What?" Harry exclaimed.

The barbeque fork clattered noisily to the patio.

"Dead?" Mike said softly.

"Drowned," his wife answered. "Vivi found him."

"I don't believe it," Mike whispered. "Where is he?"

"Down on the dock," Linda replied.

"Let's go," he said, ripping off his apron and tossing it on the table.

"You'd better turn off the barbeque first," Harry suggested, searching for the shut-off valve.

He looked at her and then at the steaks. "You're right," he replied, watching as she closed the gas. "We might not get to these tonight."

Linda led them around the cottage, through the dense stand of trees and down the path to the beach. Harry could see that the others had already gathered there – Vivi protectively tucked between Dan and Betty, Margaret and Eddie standing a bit off to the side. Everyone was staring at the human form lying motionless at the end of the dock.

"Harry!" Vivi sobbed, falling into Harry's arms.

"There, there," Betty said, patting Vivi on the back as if she was dealing with one of her children.

"I'm all right," Vivi assured them, disentangling herself from Harry. "I really am. It was just so horrible, seeing him floating in the water like that and realizing he was dead."

"He must have fallen in and drowned," Dan said with a sigh.

"But it's not deep enough," Linda protested. "It only comes up to your neck at high tide, and the tide's just halfway in right now."

"It was divine retribution," Teresa droned. "He was a sinner."

"Oh, shut up!" Harry said angrily. How could Teresa have the insensitivity to say something so vicious when Wayne was lying there dead? He could be a jerk sometimes, but nobody deserved to die for that. "Why don't you take a hike?" she added, spinning around to give Teresa the benefit of her nastiest look.

"What are we going to do?" Margaret asked, breaking the silence.

"Call the police," Harry said more harshly than she had intended.

"What?" Linda protested, glancing at Wayne's body. "Do we really have to? It was an accident."

"Yes, we really have to," Harry said.

"Somebody should cover him up," Vivi said, shuddering.

"Harriet's right; we've got to contact the police," Mike said. "I'll go call Sandy Burns."

"Sandy Burns is a cop?" Harry asked incredulously. "*Our* Sandy Burns?"

"Yup," Mike replied with the ghost of a smile. "Police chief, actually. Kind of ironic, isn't it? He would have been here tonight, but he had to work. Anyway, I'd better go call him. He won't be pleased if we wait too long to get in touch with him, even it if was an accident."

"What do you mean, *even if*?" Vivi protested.

"It was just a figure of speech," Mike said hastily.

"I'm sure it was just an accident," Betty said.

"We all had good reason to dislike Wayne, but that was years ago," Eddie said flatly.

"In another life, really," Linda added.

"And you didn't like him any better than the rest of us," Vivi said to Mike.

"Hold on, here – I didn't say it wasn't an accident," Mike objected. "All I said was that it was ironic that Sandy was the chief of police."

"Actually, he didn't like Wayne either, did he?" Vivi asked thoughtfully.

"I really couldn't say," Linda replied.

"We seem to be going around in circles," Harry commented. It sounded as if everyone had disliked Wayne, although Harry didn't know what specific reasons each of them had. But whatever he had done, hadn't it happened decades ago? Wasn't it high time to forget, if not forgive? Perhaps some of them had been in touch with Wayne in the intervening years. But if Vivi was any indication, no one would want to talk about that. What had it been about Wayne that engendered such secrecy?

"I'm guess I'd better go call Sandy," Mike said hesitantly. He glanced at the body on the dock and sprinted across the beach. Perhaps he had been hoping that Wayne would jump to his feet, point at them, and shout, "Gotcha again!" It would have been just like him.

How on earth had Sandy Burns become chief of police, even in a village like Spruce Bay? And what would happen if a serious crime was ever committed, Harry wondered as she watched Mike disappear into the copse of trees between the beach and the cottage. Sandy had been the dumbest kid in their class, and he had absolutely no sense of humour.

"Who pulled Wayne out?" Harry asked.

"I did," Dan said, stepping forward. Harry noticed for the first time that his clothes were wet. "I heard Vivi calling for help and went to see what was wrong," he explained. "I tried to pull him up on the dock, but his clothes were soaked and weighing him down, so, in the end, I had to wade out into the water and climb up the ladder with him."

"All by yourself?" Harry asked.

"It's a short ladder," Dan answered. "Three or four steps. And he didn't weigh that much. I tried to revive him, but it didn't do any good. He must have been in the water too long."

"I'll bet he was drunk and fell in and hit his head," Vivi said suddenly.

"You're probably right," Linda agreed at once. "We were all rather soused, weren't we?"

"Speak for yourself," Vivi retorted with a shaky laugh. "To tell you the truth, I've never felt so sober in my life."

"I wouldn't doubt we could all use a drink right now," Dan said with a self-conscious chuckle.

"And a steak," Vivi added. "I'm famished."

"How can you even think about food at a time like this?" Margaret exclaimed.

"It's my stomach talking," Vivi apologized, "and it won't shut up. So, sue me."

There was general hilarity, the uncontrollable mirth born of relief – relief that someone else was dead and *they* were alive. In the final analysis, that was all that mattered. Even Harry couldn't stop herself from chuckling. But briefly, she rationalized, just briefly, out of respect for the dead.

"We might as well wait inside for the police to get here," Linda said.

Harry volunteered to stay with the body, and watched as one by one, the rest of them followed Linda from the beach. She waited until they were out of sight and then walked onto the dock until she was close to Wayne's body. She forced herself to kneel, to look. It was dark, but she could see that his face was dry and slightly puffy. There was a cut on the side of his forehead, a cut and several scratches. His expression was serene, innocent, and only then did she realize that Wayne didn't look sardonic and world-weary.

"Oh, lord," she sighed, staring into his dead eyes. "What did life do to you?" She placed fingers over his cold eyelids and lowered them over his unseeing eyes. "Rest in peace, Wayne. Rest in peace."

Chapter 6

"I've never met such a jerk," Vivi said viciously as she fastened her seatbelt. "If he had a couple of ideas in his seemingly vacant mind, he might be dangerous! God! How could he have changed so much? Or has this small-town mentality finally fried his brains?"

"Shhh!" Harry said, worried that Dan and Betty would be offended.

"It's all right," Dan assured her. "I know what she means."

"We both do," Betty added.

"Well, Sandy did act rather strange," Harry admitted.

"Yeah, like he had something sharp up his –"

Harry cut Vivi off with an elbow to her ribs. "Never mind," she hissed in her ear.

"I think he was a little nervous about meeting all of you again," Betty explained. "What with having to be there in his official capacity and all."

"I know Sandy wasn't particularly impressive to start with, but then, the years haven't exactly been good to him," Dan added.

"His wife left him last winter. She just took the kids and walked out without leaving him a note or anything," Betty explained, turning around in the passenger seat to look at Harry and Vivi. "The next day, he got a lawyer's letter suing him for the house, the car, the cottage, and every last nickel in their joint bank account."

"He probably deserved it," Vivi muttered.

"Well, maybe he did, maybe he didn't," Dan replied calmly. "But it was still hard on him."

"Nobody knows what goes on in somebody else's relationship," Betty said.

"True enough," Vivi admitted, crossing her arms in front of her. "But he didn't have to be so officious. After all, we didn't do anything wrong. And once upon a time we were friends."

"Sandy always was a bit of a bore," Harry said quietly. Tonight had been no exception, she thought with a shiver. She reached out and rolled up the window. The air was damp; at some point during the evening, while Sandy had dithered over Wayne's body and then eventually called the medical examiner, likely one of the doctors in the large town half-an-hour from Spruce Bay, fog had rolled in over the water and covered the land. The headlights of Dan and Betty's Datsun barely cut through the swirling mist, and although Dan drove slowly, Harry was relieved when they finally reached the edge of the village and blacktop with a white line down the middle replaced the winding gravel road with its deep, unforgiving ditches.

"What do you mean, a *bore*?" Vivi exclaimed. "He was stupid, Harriet, just plain stupid, and everybody knew it. If there hadn't been a conspiracy among the teachers to pass him year after year, he'd still be back in grade nine. I suppose none of them could stand the thought of having him in their class for more than one year. Unfortunately, that meant that we were saddled with him for the duration."

"Now, Vivi," Betty said mildly. "Don't be mean. He wasn't all that bad."

Dan snorted.

"Of course he was," Vivi insisted stubbornly, "and you know it. We *all* know it."

It was true, Harry thought. Sandy Burns was no intellectual heavyweight. Maybe that had certain advantages in his line of work; he wouldn't be likely to faint at the sight of blood, or see treachery where there was none, or worry about the ambiguity of being a small-town cop where your friends could easily become your customers, your suspects, your witnesses, your perpetrators. But having a stalwart but dense chief of police was nothing to brag about; on the contrary, it would be a potential liability in case of a suspicious death. Not that there was anything to worry about, because Wayne had died accidentally. His death had to be investigated because he hadn't expired in bed with his boots off, but the medical examiner would soon bring in a verdict of accidental death. Still, the evening had had a certain madcap feel to it. They had all had too much to drink, presumably because they were nervous about meeting each other after so many years. And she had this niggling sensation in the back of her mind that just wouldn't go away…

"Poor Wayne," Betty said with a sigh.

"Yes," Harry agreed. "Poor Wayne." Troublemaker that he was. Or seemed to be. Or wanted to be. After so many years, how was she to know how much was real and how much was phoney, how much truth and how much image? Of course she could ask that of all her former classmates, and no doubt there were some who would want to ask the same about her.

How unfair and capricious life was, Harry mused. Earlier in the day, Wayne had been lounging in Harry's rental car, annoying her with his contentiousness. She hadn't paid much attention when he hinted about his intention to be the blight of the reunion. She had thought that he was bragging or perhaps posing as the bad boy. Who would have thought that, six hours later, he would be dead? What had he meant when he said that some people wouldn't be very happy to see him? She should have listened. They had grown up together, and that should have meant something. Or was her guilt simply puritanically inspired – the kind of useless, senseless moral crap that her lover Judy contended clogged your emotional drains and made it difficult to get on with life. Harry didn't know and Judy wasn't there to help her decide. She could separate herself from it when she was safely ensconced in Montreal, but as soon as she travelled back to Spruce Bay, she forgot what she had learned, certainly dropped away, and doubt descended like the dark of night.

"I suppose Wayne was drunk," Dan commented as he pulled into the driveway of his house. "We all were. He did seem to be well on the way the last time I talked with him."

"Such a stupid way to die," Vivi said angrily. "He fell off the stupid dock into waist high water, hit his stupid head on one of the stupid rocks and drowned like a stupid kitten tied up in a stupid bag. I just can't believe he would be such a stupid idiot to die like that."

"I know – it was senseless, just plain senseless," Harry agreed, trying to understand why Vivi was so furious about Wayne's death when she hadn't seen Wayne for over thirty years. Supposedly. As for the rest of them, why did their dislike of Wayne seem so fresh? The gnawing feeling in the back of her mind returned.

"Let's have a drink," Vivi proposed, flinging herself through the doorway just ahead of Dan.

A weary look passed between Dan and Betty, but nevertheless Dan said, "That sounds like a great idea."

"It's late," Harry said. "The kids will be up early and I'm sure you have things to do in the morning."

"Actually, Harriet, a drink sounds wonderful after what just happened. I find myself surprisingly sober and I'm not sure I want to be," Betty interrupted.

"Precisely," Vivi exclaimed with false bravado. "Who the hell wants to be sober?"

"Brandy?" Dan asked, switching on the living room light.

"That would be fine," Harry said, although all she wanted to do was sleep. And to add insult to injury, her sinuses had started to ache the moment she had stepped into the house. She liked dogs, but this was too much.

"Brandy after vodka and tonic?" Betty groaned. "I'm going to have a mother of a hangover tomorrow."

"Aren't we all?" Vivi said with feigned exuberance. "But who cares? I need to be knocked out for the night, and this is much better than a sleeping pill."

"This woman is a genius, Dan," Betty chortled.

Either Vivi had a drinking problem, or she was terribly upset about Wayne's death, Harry thought. She sat on a child-worn sofa and felt herself sink into springless nirvana.

"What did Sandy tell you?" Vivi asked as Dan handed her a brandy snifter and poured a liberal portion of amber liquid into it.

Harry looked at Vivi, sneezed into her hand, and revised her assumptions. Perhaps brandy was merely a springboard to information. It had been used as such before, and it would be so used again. On the other hand, to drink more, Vivi might just be utilizing their common need to discuss what had happened. Why was everything so double-edged?

"Nothing, really. Sandy doesn't know much more than we do at this point. But he'll muddle through," Dan commented.

"I imagine he will," Harry remarked, holding out her brandy snifter for him to fill. "In this particular case."

'What do you mean?" Betty asked.

"What if there was a murder?" Harry replied. "Would Sandy be able to handle it?"

"You're not suggesting that Wayne was murdered, are you?" Vivi said, her voice rising.

"Of course not," Harry answered, searching through her purse for some tissues. "I was talking about a hypothetical situation."

"Well don't do that," Vivi scolded, handing her a package of tissues. "It just gets me all upset."

"About all Sandy could say for sure was that Wayne was dead," Dan added glumly.

For some reason, this was hilarious.

"Do tell," Betty said hysterically.

"It's not funny," Vivi grumbled even while she was sniggering.

"Of course not," Harry guffawed sympathetically, trying to blow her nose as she laughed.

"Sandy said he thought Wayne drowned," Dan remarked as he took a large swig of brandy.

"No kidding," Vivi said sardonically. "I mean, he's a cop; couldn't he tell us something we don't know?"

Betty started to laugh and then cut it short.

Harry got up, paced the room, and sat down again without saying anything.

"I beg your pardon?" Vivi said, staring at her.

"Nothing," Harry replied gruffly, blowing her nose again.

"I think not," Vivi asserted.

"Think what you want," Harry answered curtly. She was tired and her allergies and the brandy were giving her a headache. They were being sinfully nonchalant; a friend of theirs had died tonight and they would likely regret their callousness in the morning.

"Oh, god," Vivi murmured, setting her empty brandy snifter on the scarred wood-veneer beside the sofa. "I am so wretchedly tired."

"Let's all go to bed," Betty sighed.

No one argued; it was very late.

They went upstairs, established protocol for the use of the bathroom (Dan offered to be last one in and Harry acquiesced), said goodnight, and closed the doors to their respective bedrooms.

"I am going to sleep and sleep and sleep," Vivi said emphatically, stripping naked and slipping into a sheer negligee.

Harry wasn't sure which was more provocative.

"Aren't you going to bed?" Vivi asked.

"Of course I am," Harry replied, feeling awkward. "Do you mind sleeping with the window open? I need the fresh air for my allergies."

"Of course not," Vivi replied. "I prefer to have fresh air in the room."

Harry usually slept in the nude, and she hadn't bothered to bring pyjamas because she hadn't realized that she would be sharing a room. How was she going to take off her clothes in front of Vivi? She sat on the edge of the bed and removed her sandals.

"Come here," Vivi said seductively.

Harry turned and looked at her. "I'd better not," she replied in a husky voice.

"Suit yourself," Vivi said casually, getting into bed.

She was damned if she did and damned if she didn't, Harry ruminated. Barbra Streisand wasn't the only one with memories. But on the other hand, what about Judy? Yes, what about Judy? Harry would bet a very large amount of money that Judy wasn't sleeping alone tonight…

Harry blew her nose one last time, turned out the light, dropped her clothes to the floor and got into bed. It had been a long day, but she wasn't sleepy. The mattress sagged, although it didn't smell of boy child or puppy dog. The sheets were gritty with cookie crumbs, bits of dog biscuits, crushed cereal. They were also terminally nubby. She sighed, turned over, and felt the bottom sheet pull away, exposing the plastic liner. It was cold. "Shit," she mumbled.

"Harriet," Vivi whispered.

"Yeah," Harry replied warily.

"I can't sleep."

"Try harder."

"What do you think I've been doing?" Vivi replied.

Harry shrugged.

"I heard that," Vivi muttered.

"You did not," Harry retorted, turning over again.

"Admit it. You can't sleep either."

"What are you talking about? I am asleep," Harry claimed.

"Do you dream about me like this all the time?"

"Hoisted with my own petard," Harry said with a chuckle.

"You silly duck," Vivi said affectionately.

"Yeah, right," Harry said dryly. She heard sheets rustle and stiffened as Vivi slid in beside her. "I don't think this is a good idea."

"Well, pardon me," Vivi said, snuggling up to her. "But I don't really care what you think."

"That's what I mean," Harry said primly, trying to move away. "You only want to take advantage of me."

"Obviously," Vivi responded.

Being naked, Harry was at a definite disadvantage. Not to mention that they were in a single bed with a sagging mattress; it would have been easier to scale a mountain than to climb out of the middle of the bed.

"I need comforting, Harriet," Vivi said plaintively.

Like hell, Harry thought, feeling Vivi's arms encircle her. Vivi needed something, but it wasn't comfort! "I have a girlfriend," Harry told her.

"I don't mind," Vivi replied, her hands searching. "Will she?"

"We've been together for over eleven years," Harry said, evading the real question.

"How commendable," Vivi said with obvious insincerity. "Here. Take these."

"Gloves?" Harry said, shocked.

"Of course," Vivi replied with studied nonchalance. "I believe in being careful, don't you?"

"Well, yes," Harry sputtered. She put the gloves on and felt Vivi's hands return to her body. The touches felt different but not impossible, and Harry soon forgot about the thin layer of latex between skin and fingertips.

She wanted Vivi but was reticent. "Don't," she whispered, frightened by how aroused she was. She believed that she had relinquished her right to take a lover – that it would be hypocritical of her to become involved with another woman because she opposed Judy's affair with Sarah.

"Vivi…"

"Shhh. Stop talking and pay attention," Vivi whispered. And then she took Harry. Hard.

Harry stopped talking and paid attention. Hard.

And tried not to worry about who might be lying awake in the room under theirs, listening to the springs of the swayback mattress rock and roll. Hard.

And then she slept. Soundly.

Chapter 7

"What's that?" Vivi muttered.

"I think the marines are landing," Harry groaned as she turned over and her stiff muscles protested.

"Actually, it sounds more like someone is knocking on the door," Vivi said with a yawn. "I wonder what time it is."

"It's light outside, so it must be morning," Harry responded.

"Damn! I'm not ready to get up yet," Vivi said plaintively.

"I don't think they're going to take no for an answer," Harry said dryly as the tempo of the knocking increased.

"Did you lock the door last night?"

"I never thought about it," Harry replied, burying her head under the covers while she waited for the proverbial storm to break.

"You mean someone could have walked in on us?" Vivi sputtered, jumping out of Harry's bed as the pounding on the door got louder. "We could have been discovered! I could have been disgraced!"

"Vivi, I don't even know if the door has a lock," Harry said. And besides, you started it, she thought but didn't say.

"How could you have been so thoughtless? I mean, if my husband ever found out…" Vivi said through clenched teeth.

Harry had forgotten how mercurial Vivi could be. And she didn't want to think about the fact that Vivi had a husband. She had nearly managed to overlook him while they made love – nearly, but not quite. The gloves had made it easier. But she wouldn't have oral sex with Vivi, even though Vivi had insisted that if they split a condom down the side, it would work as well as a dental dam, but she didn't have any of them with her. Harry hadn't been willing to explain why she wouldn't have oral sex except to say that she generally didn't do it on the first date. Fortunately, Vivi had been too excited to say something sarcastic. Still, Harry had wondered why Vivi would come to her high school reunion with gloves and condoms, but she didn't ask.

"I can't believe you could be so careless," Vivi reproached her.

"Well, it didn't do any harm," Harry said. "No one paid us a midnight visit." She got out of bed, picked up her bra and panties from the floor and put them on.

Whoever was outside stopped knocking on the door and walked into the bedroom.

"I beg your pardon," Vivi said imperiously, jumping out of bed and spinning to face the intruder in all her splendid nakedness.

"Dammit, Vivi! Put on some clothes, will you?" Dan exclaimed, turning his head away.

"How dare you barge in here like this?" Vivi stormed.

"Just get dressed, will you?" Harry said as she pulled on jeans and a sweatshirt and then combed her short hair with her fingers. "What is it, Dan? Can't it wait a bit?"

"Sandy's here," Dan said.

"Did he come by to tell you that he finally realized that Wayne was dead?" Vivi said sarcastically as she zipped up her jeans and pulled a T-shirt over her head.

"Wayne was murdered," Dan muttered.

"You've got to be kidding," Vivi said, turning to face Dan. "You always did like to tease the girls. Why, I can remember some of the practical jokes you played when we were in school."

"He's not kidding, Vivi," Harry interrupted. "Are you, Dan?"

"I wish I was," Dan said quietly.

"I must be having a nightmare," Viv said. "Pinch me, Harriet."

"Be serious," Harry said reproachfully.

"Sandy has a few questions he wants to ask you," Dan said.

"Can't it wait? I'm still half asleep," Vivi complained, looking at herself in the mirror. "And look at my hair – it's a mess!"

Vivi had always been capable of drama – either she had created it, encouraged it or lived it, but Harry knew that at this very moment, Vivi was just avoiding what might be the truth. "Dan is only telling us what Sandy said – that Wayne was murdered. So now the police want to talk to us."

"Po-lice?" Vivi responded, giving the word the two-syllable pronunciation of a southern belle.

Harry had no more patience left. "I'll meet you downstairs," she said abruptly, leading Dan from the room. "I'll be damned if I know what's got into her," she said heatedly as she sneezed. "I've never seen her like this. She isn't taking anything seriously."

"Maybe she's more shocked about Wayne's death than she wants anyone to know," Dan said quietly as they went down the stairs.

Harry stopped at the bottom of the stairs and turned to look at him. "How'd you get to be so smart?"

"When you've got as many kids as we do, you've either got to learn to swim or you sink to the bottom like a stone," he answered succinctly.

"It's certainly taken you long enough to get down here," Sandy Burns complained as he approached them from the living room.

"I was still asleep," Harry replied calmly, trying not to let her dislike of him show. He was tall and pink and stoop-shouldered, a flabby excuse of a man. His muscles were slack from lack of exercise, his eyes were recessed behind excessively puffy flesh, and the skin around his thin lips was tinged with blue. There was something wrong with his heart, Harry thought. Or he had clogged arteries – a coronary ready to happen. "And it's nice to see you again, too," she added sarcastically.

"Yeah. Real nice. Where's Vivi?" Sandy asked, looking around suspiciously, as if he believed that Vivi planned to escape while he was otherwise occupied with Harry and Dan.

"She's coming," Harry replied, trying to sniff quietly. The dog must be skulking somewhere, silently sneaking close enough to make her nose run. "Shall be go into the living room? Dan told me that you have a few questions to ask me."

"Yes, actually, I do," he replied, following Harry into the living room while glancing worriedly behind him. "Dan, you'll make sure that Vivi comes right in."

"Sure," Dan said.

Harry sat on the sofa and watched Sandy pace in front of the fireplace. "So, Harriet. Wayne was murdered," he said bluntly. "What do you think about that?"

"I think it's horrible," Harry answered. She pulled her legs up under her; the house was damp, and her bare feet were cold.

Sandy stopped pacing and looked at her. "What do you mean?"

"Just that," she said with a sigh. Was Sandy so unsure of himself that he doubted the meaning of what everyone said? What a conundrum for a policeman. People were predisposed to telling the truth some of the time, even to a cop. "But how do you know he was murdered?"

"Doc Harris said there wasn't any water in his lungs," Sandy replied.

"Then he was dead before he hit the water," Harry reflected, dredging a half-used tissue from her pocket and using it to blow her nose. Where was that damned dog? Or was the dog hair littered about the house enough to trigger her allergies?

"How do you know?" Sandy asked suspiciously, approaching the sofa.

"Anybody who's read a lot of detective stories would know that," Harry explained patiently. Did he really think she was a suspect? "How did he die?"

"Somebody hit him on the head, probably with a piece of wood. He was pushed into the water after he was dead," Sandy replied.

"How long after?"

"Doc Harris said it was hard to know for sure. But not too long," Sandy answered. "All we know is that someone killed him."

"Alexander Burns, do you mean to stand there and tell me that Wayne Williams was *murdered*?" Vivi said dramatically as she swept into the living room and perched on the edge of an upholstered easy chair.

"That's precisely what I'm saying," Sandy said without bothering to look at Vivi.

Did Vivi have to pinch his butt to get his attention, Harry wondered with amusement. Vivi would not be pleased.

"And I suppose you think that one of us must have killed him," Vivi added with a laugh which indicated that anyone who thought that was clearly deluded.

"It had occurred to me," Sandy replied soberly.

Harry sneezed and then leaned back and looked at Vivi, who was silent for a change.

"I've asked the RCMP to help with this," Sandy added self-importantly. "It's a bit too much for me to handle alone. My deputies aren't real policemen, they haven't had much training, not like I have. And there's a lot to do in a case like this. We've already searched Wayne's motel room, but we didn't find anything unusual. I want to know about your movements of last night and find out whether any of you were in touch with Wayne since we graduated. There were ten of you at the cottage, after all. Well, nine, not counting Wayne."

"I can see that's a lot for one person to do," Harry commented as she blew her nose. Perhaps the presence of the RCMP would result in some real progress being made.

"So why don't you tell me what you did at the barbecue?" Sandy asked Harry.

Harry did, in as few words as possible.

"And you never saw Wayne after your initial conversation with him just after you arrived and dropped him at the motel?"

"No," Harry replied.

"Me neither," Vivi said voluntarily.

"Well, where was he?" Sandy asked.

"I don't know," Harry answered. "Maybe he was down on the beach."

"I'm surprised he didn't spend more time in the house," Sandy commented. "That seems to be where everyone else congregated."

"That's where all the booze was," Vivi remarked with a short laugh.

"Well, somebody must have seen him," Sandy said. "I'm sure I'll find out. In the meantime, you can't leave town," he added, picking up his hat from the coffee table.

"But that's not fair," Vivi responded plaintively. "Perhaps it wasn't one of us – I mean, you can't prove that it was!"

"Not yet," Sandy replied stiffly.

"Don't be silly," Vivi scoffed. "It could have been anyone. Maybe it was one of our classmates who wasn't at the barbecue but who arrived last night. Or a classmate who lives here, like you. Or someone else from the village who decided to take the opportunity to do him in. Wayne must have had a lot of enemies – you know what he was like."

"No, I don't," Sandy replied. "Why don't you tell me?"

Harry flinched, but Vivi was quick to see the trap he had set for her. "Now, now," she said, wagging her finger at him.

"You can't have forgotten what a pest he was in high school, or how he just loved to be mean to everyone. He was a real bully when he got carried away."

Sandy studied Vivi's face, and then turned to Harry. "Do you have anything else to say about this?"

"No," she said, shaking her head. "I already told you that I gave him a lift from the airport in Halifax."

He nodded. "Yeah, you did. Well, I guess that's about it for now. But I'll want to talk to the both of you again."

"What on earth for? We've told you everything," Vivi said.

"No one ever tells me *everything*," Sandy murmured. "No one."

He was right, Harry thought as she unsuccessfully searched her pockets for another tissue. She herself had omitted part of the conversation she and Wayne had had on the drive from Halifax to Spruce Bay. She hadn't told Sandy that Wayne had gloated about how unhappy some of his old classmates were going to be when they saw him. She asked herself, not for the first time, which of their classmates he had been referring to. She hadn't inquired, and Wayne hadn't said. In fact, he had seemed to take pleasure in hoarding this information. Harry could nearly visualize him wrapping it around his body like something soft and furry and comforting.

"Think about it and see if you can remember anything else that might be important," Sandy droned.

"We will," Harry said with a nod and watched him leave the room. Shortly after she heard a door slam.

"What a bore," Vivi said.

"He's just doing his job," Harry contended reasonably. "Have you got a tissue? My allergies are killing me."

"Since when did you start defending jerks like him?" Vivi asked ferociously. "And no, I don't have any tissues left. You'll have to sniff."

"I don't understand where you're coming from," Harry said, sniffing as quietly as she could.

"Well, perhaps you can understand where I'm going, then," Vivi said with saccharine intonation. "I'm simply exhausted, so I'm going back to bed."

Had she really made love with this woman? "What on earth is the matter with you, Vivi? You're not making any sense."

Vivi said something unintelligible and ran from the room, nearly knocking Betty down.

"I'd better go after her," Harry told Betty as she rose from the sofa.

"Be careful," Betty said, grasping her arm.

"Do you know something I don't?" Harry asked her.

"About Vivi? Not really, but I can certainly guess," Betty replied with a knowing smile.

"And about me?" Harry couldn't resist asking.

"Don't be silly," Betty answered, releasing her hold on Harry's arm. "I don't even have to guess about that. In any case, perhaps Vivi needs to be alone right now."

Harry controlled her impulse to run after Vivi. Betty could be right, and she wasn't sure she could deal with Vivi's petulance without losing her temper.

"You seem to know a surprising amount about people," Harry remarked with another sniff. "What do you know about Wayne?"

"No more than anyone else, and perhaps less than some," Betty replied evasively.

"Things are as clear as mud," Harry muttered. She felt as if she had fallen down the rabbit hole. These people she had once known intimately were no longer who they had been. She had spent years in their presence, and she had adored some and detested others with the strong, fresh passion uniquely exhibited by the young. She had fully expected her memories to fade, to be somewhat askew, but it had never occurred to her that they would be false. She was disconcerted that Vivi, who had always been so empathetic, appeared not to care about anyone but herself, while Betty, who had been as transparent as glass, was acting like a sphinx.

"If you ask me, everybody there last night had a secret," Betty said with a knowing smile. "You included."

"We all have our secrets," Harry said, "although mine seems to be less confidential than most."

"A secret about Wayne, I mean," Betty patiently corrected her. "Hasn't is occurred to you that Sandy is likely right? That one of us killed him?"

"Of course it has," Harry admitted. "We were there, after all. We had the most opportunity."

"And one of us has a secret which is not so innocent, a secret which he or she would do anything to protect," Betty said in a low tone.

"It would seem so," Harry replied.

"Oh, lord, Sandy will never discover who it was," Betty sighed. "Neither will our illustrious RCMP constable, for that matter. I think Roger Dalton and Sandy Burns must have studied at the same police college. All the two of them will do is compete to see who's the most stupid."

"How inspirational," Harry remarked.

"Quite," Betty answered with a dry laugh. "On that note, I think I'll go make breakfast. Children are like little animals, especially in the beginning. In one end and out the other, and that's about the truth of it. At least the oldest ones can fend for themselves now, although there are all sorts of new things to worry about. Violence in the schools, drugs, HIV – but you wouldn't know about that, would you?"

"As a teacher, not a parent," Harry replied.

"Of course," Betty said, clearly dismissing her limited experience. "I'll be off, then."

"Want some help?"

"To be honest, I've got it down to such a routine that you'd probably just get in the way," Betty said. "See you in a bit."

Harry nodded, returned to the living room and stretched out on the sofa. She was tired and wanted to sleep, but she was reluctant to return to the room she and Vivi were sharing even though she knew her allergies would be more under control if she did. She didn't think she could stand to hear one more of Vivi's grievances, not when Wayne was lying on a mortician's slab trussed like a turkey after having been sliced open by the medical examiner.

Wayne was dead. Murdered. Warm flesh and blood and intelligence rudely cut down in cold blood. Harry had been there when it had happened, but she didn't have a clue who had killed him. And if Betty was right, the town police and the RCMP would be incapable of discovering who the murderer was. Eventually they would give up. Wayne's body would be released and buried in the Spruce Bay cemetery. She would be permitted to return to Montreal, Vivi to Toronto. Life would go on; no matter what the personal catastrophe, it always did. Eventually

Wayne's untimely death would fade from memory. A murderer would go free, unpunished.

She had to prevent that from happening, she thought sleepily. After all, it hadn't been that long since she had successfully unravelled the mystery surrounding the death of an elderly motel owner on Cape Cod, and she was more intelligent than Sandy Burns, more determined to get to the bottom of it. So be it, then. She would do her best, she decided as her eyes closed, and she drifted off to sleep.

Chapter 8

A wet, raspy tongue licked Harry's face. She warily opened her eyes to see Frisky sitting on her chest, whimpering and wagging his tail.

"Just what I need," she groaned with a sneeze, reaching up to push the puppy away.

"Did you sleep here all night?" asked Bert as he padded into the living room.

"No. I got up earlier and then I fell asleep on the couch," Harry answered, sitting up to search for a tissue.

"My dad does that sometimes when he's had too much to drink," Bert confided, sitting down beside her. Frisky jumped into his lap and began licking him on the face.

"You shouldn't let him do that," Harry said, sneezing again.

"Why not?" Bert asked, hugging the dog to him.

"Germs."

"I don't care," Bert said. "Did you have too much to drink?"

"No," Harry answered.

"That's what my dad always says," Bert mused.

Out of the mouths of babes, Harry thought, blowing her nose, which was starting to get sore.

"Bert, do you know where Mom's gone?" asked a young man.

"Nope," Bert replied without looking at the older boy. "Were you drunk, though?" he asked Harry.

"No, I wasn't," Harry replied absently, staring at the young man. He had long, black, wavy hair and was handsome in a sulky way. "I'm Harriet Hubbley, a classmate of your parents," she said to him.

"Charles," he responded. "Better known as Chip."

"You're Betty and Dan's eldest son," Harry said, looking more closely at him. He reminded her of someone, but she didn't know who. He certainly didn't look like either of his parents, or the two children she had already met.

"That's right," he said in a bored voice.

Harry decided that she didn't much like him.

"Anyway, when you see Mom, tell her I've gone out," Chip said to Bert.

"Sure," said Bert as he cuddled Frisky.

"Do you have any idea what time it is?" Harry asked Bert after Chip left the room.

"Nope," Bert said. "I don't have a watch yet. Mommy says I'm too young. Will you buy me one?"

"Maybe," Harry prevaricated, not sure exactly what to say.

"Hey, cool!" Bert exclaimed as he jumped from the sofa. The puppy landed on the floor and dashed from the room. "Ever neat! Can I pick it out?"

"I said maybe, not yes," Harry asserted, but the boy wasn't listening. He ran out of the room before she could protest further. The hell with it, she thought; she would get him one of those cheap watches that kids seemed to like, and that would be that. The next time she would know better than to say maybe when no was the right answer.

"So here you are," Vivi remarked, walking swiftly into the room and sitting beside Harry. "Why didn't you come back to our room? I was waiting for you." She was dressed in a pink sweatshirt and pink pants. Even her running shoes were pink. Harry thought rather uncharacteristically that she probably had lipstick and fingernail polish which were the same shade, and then felt ashamed of herself. One of the reasons she had been attracted to Vivi had been her femininity, so it wasn't fair to deride it now.

"I fell asleep on the sofa," Harry replied, not certain how to explain to Vivi that she needed some distance between herself and everyone else. She suspected that Vivi wouldn't be capable of seeing herself as being in that category.

Vivi studied her expression and then looked away. "What's going to happen now? Are we just supposed to sit around and wait for the police to tell us we can go home?"

"I don't know," Harry said, and then she sneezed.

"Want to hear what I think?" Betty asked, walking into the room. Dan was behind her. "We should continue with our reunion. That's what Wayne would have wanted us to do."

"I think Betty's right," Harry said slowly, although she had no idea what Wayne would have wanted. But it would serve no tangible purpose to cancel everything. And, if she was going to find out who had murdered Wayne, she would have to ask questions. She would be less conspicuous if they continued to hold whatever events had been planned.

"Don't you think that would be disrespectful?" Vivi asked, sounding annoyed.

"Not really," Harry replied. "We have to stay here, so we might as well stick together."

"You don't think that we're in any danger, do you?" Vivi asked, her voice suddenly alert.

"What?" Harry exclaimed. "Of course not! I didn't mean it that way."

"Of course she didn't," Betty said soothingly. "Harry means that we'd probably feel better if we didn't sit around doing nothing."

"Exactly," Harry replied even though she wasn't sure it was true. Vivi had alerted her to another possibility, though, one which hadn't occurred to her before. Had Wayne been the only victim, or was he simply the first?

"I've spoken with some of the others this morning, and everyone agrees," Betty said, turning to Dan for confirmation.

"We've cancelled the softball game this afternoon," Dan replied. "No one felt much like fooling around. But people would like to proceed with the walking tour of the town and school later this morning and the dinner dance tonight. We already paid for the yacht club, the catering service and the band, so we decided to go ahead with it rather than lose our money."

"Well, I don't know about partying," Vivi remarked.

"And then there's the ecumenical church service tomorrow morning at the United Church," Betty said hastily. "I'm sure Mike will say a few words about Wayne. After that, Linda and Mike have offered to have an informal, late-afternoon get-together at their cottage."

"I still don't think we should do anything," Vivi opined stubbornly. "Socialize together in small groups, but that's all. It's not appropriate."

"Well, I don't agree," Betty said, turning to Dan for support.

"Neither do I," Harry added, wondering when Vivi had started to worry about what was appropriate.

"I don't know about you, but I'm going to get ready," Betty said. "We're supposed to be at the post office in half an hour."

"I'll go on the walk, but that's all," Vivi muttered as she rose from the sofa.

"What's the matter with you, Vivi?" Dan asked impatiently.

"I don't know what you're talking about," Vivi insisted haughtily, brushing past him. "You must be imagining things."

As Betty and Vivi left the room, Dan turned and looked at Harry. "Do *you* think I'm imagining things?"

Harry blew her nose again and shrugged. "Right now, I'm not sure I'd know if *I* was imagining things."

He snorted, but not because he was amused. "What do you think's happening?" he asked quietly.

"What makes you so sure I know anything?" Harry said. She tucked the saturated tissue into her pocket and searched for another.

"You've been awfully quiet this morning. And you were last night, too," he replied, sitting beside her on the sofa. "When you got that look on your face when we were in high school, you usually knew exactly what was going on."

"Well, you're wrong," she told him with a laugh. "I haven't the faintest. Besides, I'm too busy dealing with my allergy to your dog to think about much else. Have you got a tissue, by any chance?"

He looked disappointed. "You can have my hanky," he said, reaching in his back pocket, pulling out a cloth handkerchief and handing it to her.

"Do *you* know something?" Harry asked curiously. She felt reluctant to blow her nose on the starched, ironed handkerchief, but in the end, she had to.

He shifted his wiry body, ran his hand through thinning hair and grimaced. "I hope you don't think I'm silly," he replied. "After all, I never went any further than high school and even then, I barely squeaked through grade twelve. I believe they let me graduate because they wanted to see the last of me, just like they did with Sandy. And I've never done anything but fish all my life. But I've been thinking about who might have killed Wayne," Dan continued. "You saw what kind of religious nut Teresa Middleton is. She's such a fanatic that she sounds almost crazy sometimes. What if she and Wayne had a run-in at Mike and Linda's? He would have really enjoyed baiting her, and if she was pushed far enough, she might have killed him. You heard what she said down on the beach last night."

"That Wayne's death was divine retribution," Harry said thoughtfully.

"And that he was a fornicator and a sinner," Dan added.

"That's true – and it's interesting," Harry said. "But if she's suddenly decided to bump off fornicators and sinners, there won't be many of us left by the time she's finished."

"You're right," Dan laughed.

"Actually, though, I don't think she did it," Harry said, not mentioning that she had already thought of Teresa. Religious fundamentalists weren't necessarily killers. In fact, Harry imagined that few of them were. There were some anti-abortion protestors who went too far. But born-again Christians were mainly thorns in the sides of minorities like hers and impediments to social progress.

"Why not?" Dan asked.

"It's too easy," she replied.

"Sometimes things are," he said, glancing at his watch. "Anyway, I'd better get ready."

"Me, too," Harry said, rising from the sofa. "Dan, I think I'm going to move out."

He looked surprised.

"Nothing personal," Harry hastened to assure him. "I just need my own space. And my allergies are getting worse."

"I guess it's pretty hard living with so many kids when you're not used to it," Dan said as they left the living room.

"Yes, it is," Harry replied, even though she was more interested in separating herself from Vivi and Frisky than in leaving Betty and Dan's cluttered house.

"You'd better get changed," Vivi said when Harry entered their room. "We're going to be late if you don't hurry up."

"I'm going to move out," Harry told her.

"What the hell are you talking about?" Vivi asked. She had changed into blue jeans and a long-sleeved white blouse with a denim vest.

"I'm going to rent a room at the Barnacle Motel," Harry said, tossing her suitcase on the unmade bed. If they had a vacancy, she thought. But she couldn't stay here, that was certain. If there were no rooms at the Barnacle, she would drive further afield to find a motel that had space for her.

"I see," Vivi said sulkily, throwing herself between Harry and the bed.

"Let me pack, Vivi!" Harry protested.

"Why are you rejecting me?" Vivi demanded.

"I'm not rejecting you," Harry said, exasperated. "I just don't want to stay here any longer. My allergies are making me sick."

"Tell me the truth! It's not the dog, it's me, isn't it?" Vivi insisted. "You think I had something to do with Wayne's death, don't you?" she added, flopping down on the bed.

Hello! This was interesting. "Of course I don't," Harry protested, pushing her suitcase to the floor and sitting down beside Vivi. Did Vivi have something to do with it? But how could she ask?

"You wouldn't be treating me like this if you didn't," Vivi responded.

"Don't be silly," Harry remonstrated gently, taking Vivi's hand in hers.

"You really don't think I did?"

"Of course not!"

"Really?" Vivi asked, peering up at Harry.

"Really," Harry said, holding back a sigh. What a childlike response, she thought; Vivi hadn't grown up at all. "I don't think you told me everything, but that doesn't mean that you killed Wayne."

"Then why are you being like this all of a sudden?" Vivi asked morosely.

She's got you there, Harry mused, not certain how to respond. She could tell the truth and reveal her guilt about being unfaithful to Judy even though Judy was being unfaithful to her. But then, she and Judy had agreed to drop the old terminology; they would no longer use words like adultery, infidelity, promiscuity. Rather, they would speak of having an open relationship. Judy seemed to believe that this was fundamentally different from being unfaithful, but Harry had difficulty telling one from the other. She hadn't been able to grasp the concept, especially emotionally. She had agreed because she hadn't wanted to lose Judy, whom she loved dearly. That her compliance enabled her to bed other women was a bonus about which she was remarkably ambivalent.

"It can't be that complicated," Vivi said. "Why can't you tell me?"

And Vivi had a husband. Why hadn't she thought about that last night? The thought of making love to a woman in a sexual relationship with a man repulsed her, and Harry had never been tempted to become involved with a bisexual woman. Last night had simply been a case of succumbing to old desires, old memories. She had been passionately attracted to Vivi when they were teenagers, but she had been a fool to think that Vivi would be the same woman she had been three decades ago and perhaps even more of a fool to suppose that making love with Vivi would assuage old longings. Teenage lust was but a memory, one she should have left in the past where it belonged.

"Harriet, tell me the truth!" Vivi insisted impatiently.

The truth was she Harry didn't particularly like the present-day incarnation of Bridget "Vivi" Andrews.

"Well, say something – you owe it to me!" Vivi exclaimed.

"I'm moving out because I'd feel more comfortable staying in a room at the Barnacle Motel," Harry replied, evading the whole truth.

"But why don't you want to stay with me?"

"It has nothing to do with you," Harry fibbed with a sneeze. Well, at least it was only a partial lie. "My allergies are driving me crazy. It's the dog. And the dust."

Vivi opened her mouth and closed it again.

"And I did tell you I had a girlfriend," Harry reminded her.

"Yes, but you didn't kick me out of your bed," Vivi replied with a seductive smile.

How regrettably true, Harry through ruefully. "I should have, though," she answered gently.

"Oh, Harriet," Vivi sighed, leaning toward her.

"When was the last time you saw Wayne?" Harry whispered as Vivi put her arms around her.

"You're just trying to take advantage of me!" Vivi said plaintively, rising from the bed.

"What are you talking about?" Harry asked. "You've obviously seen Wayne since we graduated from high school. Why have you been lying about it?"

"I'm not the only one who's seen him," Vivi said viciously.

"That may be, but you're the one I'm asking at this very moment," Harry retorted impatiently.

Vivi cursed under her breath and sat back down on the bed. "You always did know me too well," she said, giving Harry a spurious smile. "You're right. I confess. I did run into Wayne in Toronto."

"Tell me about it," Harry prodded, taking Vivi's hand again and feeling like a cad.

"I met him shortly after I moved to Toronto. Wayne wasn't the only one who had dreams about being an actor, although I never mentioned my aspirations to anyone in Spruce Bay. I didn't want to get laughed out of town, or for people to think that I had failed," Vivi confided. "I suppose I had more of a sense of reality than Wayne. I mean, he really thought he was going to make it."

"So he told me," Harry said.

"He was a real bastard," Vivi continued. "I never liked him in school, but you know how it is. When you live in a tiny village like this, you put up with your classmates because you don't have any other choice. I wasn't pleased to see him again in Toronto. I suppose it was inevitable, though. We were both auditioning for the same plays. Neither of us had much success. And then I met my first husband, married him, and started having babies."

"Did you see Wayne after that?" Harry asked.

"Unfortunately, yes. He was a good friend of my first husband, who fancied himself a serious actor because he had once had a speaking part in a play which bombed after a couple of weeks," Vivi said in an acerbic voice. "I saw Wayne less frequently once I was divorced, but he insisted on coming around. He said we were old pals from the same town, and we should stay in touch. He was such a slimy character! He was always broke and trying to sponge money. He never believed that I had less than he did. Other times he was strung out and needed a place to crash for a day or two."

"He took drugs?"

"Don't look at me like that," Vivi told her. "That's one thing I've never done. Wayne became a real annoyance once I got married again. My second husband is rather old-fashioned. Among other things, he doesn't think that it's proper for a woman to have close male friends. And believe you me, I've been quite willing to accommodate him. I was sick and tired of being poor. I told Wayne to get out of my hair, but it was like shouting at the side of a barn."

"When did you last see him?" Harry inquired, wondering how to ask Vivi whether their relationship had ever been sexual. She tried to remember whether Vivi and Wayne had dated in high school, but she couldn't recall. Vivi had been popular, and to a love-stricken Harry, it had seemed that she had gone out with every boy in the county at least once, but she couldn't recall if Wayne had been on that long, long list.

"Oh, I can't quite recall when he last dropped by," Vivi said, releasing Harry's hand.

Harry knew at once that Vivi way lying. "Was he bothering you? Threatening you in some way?"

"Don't be foolish," Vivi said, glancing at her watch and standing up. "He was just a pest. My goodness, look at the time! And you're not even dressed yet. I think it would be better if I met you there, don't you?"

"You're such a bad liar," Harry said bluntly.

"Aren't I, though? But I didn't kill him, if that's what you're wondering," Vivi responded, giving Harry a charming smile as she left the room and closed the door behind her.

She hadn't discovered whether Vivi and Wayne had been sexually involved with each other, Harry thought with a sigh. That would have to come later. But for sure there had been more going on than Vivi had been willing to admit. She threw her clothes into her suitcase and took it out to the car with her.

Chapter 9

How many others had lied about having been in contact with Wayne in the three decades since they had graduated from high school, Harry wondered as she drove her rental car from Betty and Dan's house to the post office. Perhaps he had been killed because of something he had done or said during those years, or maybe his death had been motivated by something which had occurred since he had arrived in Spruce Bay. If so, there certainly hadn't been much time for said occurrence to develop into murderous intent, Harry thought.

She pulled into a parking space beside the boarded-up movie theatre, turned off the ignition and got out of her car. At least her nose had stopped running and her sinuses hardly ached. It was just as well she had decided to move into the motel – she didn't think her system could stand a whole weekend of sneezing and nose-blowing.

"I thought you weren't going to show up," Betty said, running over to Harry as she approached the small group gathered in front of the post office. "Dan mentioned to me what he told you about Teresa, and that you didn't think she was a suspect."

"We're all suspects, as far as that goes," Harry replied.

"That's what I told Dan, but he finds it hard to think someone could suspect him of murder. I suppose we all do," Betty said with a laugh.

"How true," Harry replied as Betty gave her a hug and rushed off.

"How are you this morning?" Linda asked, taking Harry's arm in hers. She was wearing a white halter which contrasted with her tanned skin and revealed more cleavage than Harry had seen in recent memory. She tried to keep her eyes from straying in that direction with sporadic success.

"Fine," Harry replied.

"Wonderful," Linda remarked, squeezing Harry's arm. "Is this tour ever going to start, or are we going to stand here in the sun all morning?"

"I hope not," Harry replied. "I didn't think to put on any suntan lotion."

"Besides, I see this damn street every other day," Linda grumbled, "so what in hell am I doing here?"

"Communing with your classmates," Harry said offhandedly.

"Oh right! Thanks for reminding me," Linda replied with mock cheerfulness.

"When we were driving down here yesterday, Wayne said he was looking forward to seeing you again," Harry lied casually.

Linda turned and scrutinized Harry's face for several seconds, her expression impartial.

"And don't tell me that you don't know what I mean," Harry added for good measure. If she was going to be outrageous, she might as well go all the way.

"What else did he say?" Linda asked, removing her arms from Harry's so she could turn to face her.

"Enough. You know Wayne; he could never keep things to himself," Harry replied, watching Linda place her hand on her hip and put all her weight on one leg. She looked exactly like that insolent, in-your-face teenager who had infuriated their teachers with her bold stare and tarty clothes. Some of them had probably been intimidated, too, Harry decided on reflection, especially the male ones. And with good reason.

"Damn that bastard," Linda fumed. "He couldn't keep his mouth shut, even when it was in his own best interest."

Harry remained silent.

"Well, there's no point in denying it, is there?" Linda concluded.

"Not really," Harry replied, desperately trying to think of a way to get Linda to be more specific.

"Of course, he was just one of many when we were in high school," Linda resumed. "And for all his reputation as a lady's man, he was a surprisingly lousy lay."

"Let's walk over this way," Harry suggested. Margaret Ross and Eddie Foster were fast approaching, and she didn't want them butting in at such a crucial point in their conversation.

"Wayne was a jerk," Linda told her as they walked past the movie theatre. "He didn't seem very interested in sex, although that was all he ever talked about in that dirty way of his. When I look back on it now, I don't think he had much respect for women."

Harry glanced behind them and was relieved to see that Margaret and Eddie had stopped to talk with Betty and Vivi.

"But you saw him after we graduated from high school, didn't you," she stated.

"He must have told you all about that," Linda replied suspiciously.

"I want to hear it from you," Harry said, thinking fast. "You know how Wayne bragged about things. I'd like to be certain I've got it right."

"Of course! How could I forget how much he loved to exaggerate?" Linda said with a disillusioned laugh. "Well, it's not all that complicated. Likely nearly everybody, Wayne came back to Spruce Bay occasionally. He always called me, and at first, I said no. I was being the good parson's wife, you know, all peaches and cream and smiles and being pleasant to Mike's parishioners and going to every service and all the rest of that crap. But it soured on me, Harriet, it really did."

"I understand," Harry said. What an unenviable life, she thought.

"I knew you would," Linda said. "You were lucky – you got out of Spruce Bay in time. When I married Mike, I thought I was escaping too. And for a while I did. He and I had a fine time together. He was wild, as wild as me, and it was wonderful. Life was one big party. Then something horrible happened. He became religious and that destroyed my life."

"It must have been quite a shock," Harry commented sympathetically as they rounded the corner at the far end of the theatre. She could see the harbour from there. The water in the bay was deep blue and a few trawlers were sailing out to sea.

"Shocked isn't the right word," Linda said. "At first, I thought I'd divorce him, but I couldn't figure out what to do after that. I mean, like a lot of girls who were sure they were going to get married, I never bothered to get trained to do anything. I never thought I'd end up working. Now I've got this job waiting on customers in one of the clothing stores on Main Street, but that doesn't pay much. I certainly couldn't support myself on it. And back then, I hadn't ever worked, so I was afraid that I would end up on welfare."

"Then you decided to make the most of it," Harry said.

"Yes," Linda confirmed. "But I don't think I'll ever understand what happened to Mike."

"What do you mean?" Harry asked.

"One day Mike was himself, planning some deviltry or other, and the next day he was a stranger," Linda explained. "It was like he was reborn as a Christian overnight. At least that's the way he rationalizes it. He doesn't try to explain it; when you ask him about it, he says something like 'thank the Lord,' and dammit, he's serious! How could something like that happen to my husband?"

"I don't know," Harry admitted.

"He really ruined my life," Linda said. "I married one man and ended up with another. Can you blame me for having a little fun?"

"You mean with Wayne," Harry stated.

"Among others," Linda conceded.

But Harry wasn't interested in them. "Had you been with Wayne recently?"

"He and I were just getting dressed when you and Vivi and Betty and Dan Richards arrived," Linda said with a laugh. "How's that for timing? Of course, you were a little early."

"How could you take such a chance?" Harry asked.

"Don't you understand? That's part of the excitement, the thrill!" Linda laughed.

"But what if Mike found out?"

"What could he do even if he did?" Linda responded.

Kill Wayne Williams, Harry thought involuntarily.

"Do you think Mike would divorce me at this point?" Linda asked, tugging at Harry's arm. "Think what it would do to his career."

She was right, Harry thought. "But does he know?"

"I don't rub his nose in it, if that's what you mean," Linda responded. "I try to keep it as quiet as possible."

They had walked around the block and were drawing near to their classmates.

"I hope you do understand," Linda said with some urgency, "because it's the truth. And I don't want you to think badly of me. I'm just doing what I need to do to survive."

"You know everyone here, Linda. Just out of curiosity, who do you think would want to kill Wayne?" Harry asked.

"Oh, hell, Harriet, any one of us," Linda exclaimed. "Take a good look around and tell me whether you can count anyone out."

Harry looked around silently.

Betty and Dan Richards were deep in conversation with Vivi, who gave Harry a brief injured look before turning back to the Richards to say something. Harry was glad she had taken the time to pack her suitcase after Vivi had stormed from their room. It was now in the trunk of her rental car, and as soon as the tour was over, she planned to drive to the Barnacle Motel. Mike Schmidt was dressed casually, although he was wearing his clerical collar. He was chatting with Eddie Foster and Margaret Ross, both of whom were dressed in shorts and shirts. For a second, Harry debated which of them had the worst legs, then berated herself for being uncharitable.

She was surprised to see that Teresa Middleton had graced the reunion with her presence. She was listening to Police Chief Burns, who was holding forth at great length to a young, dark-haired man Harry supposed was Constable Roger Dalton.

There were others, too, people who had not attended the barbeque the night before. Harry recognized most of them and supposed those that she didn't were spouses. "Tell me why you think they're all suspects," she said to Linda in a low voice.

Linda looked at Harry and laughed. "Come on, Harriet, you were the smartest one in our class. You should be able to figure it out for yourself."

"But you've lived here all your life, while I lost contact with everyone," Harry protested, although she was secretly pleased that Linda thought she was so smart. Personally, she had never been entirely sure. "You know so much more about them than I do."

"Only about some of them," Linda corrected her. "I don't know anything about Vivi, for example, except what Wayne told me."

Of course, Harry thought excitedly. Wayne wouldn't have been able to resist telling his lovers about each other. "What did he say?"

"Oh, the usual. How she was in bed, which apparently wasn't great," Linda said with a smug smile. "Although he probably said that to everyone."

Vivi hadn't been all that bad in bed, Harry mused, although she certainly couldn't say that to Linda. "Anything else?"

"He also said that she was a complainer, that she was never satisfied with anything, and that she married her second husband for his money," Linda continued. "And after that, she didn't want to see Wayne anymore. He said he used to loan her money, and that she never paid him back."

"Funny, that's exactly what Vivi said about Wayne," Harry mused.

"Maybe they were more suited to each other than they realized," Linda giggled, and then she stopped short and put her hand over her mouth. "God! I shouldn't make fun of the dead, should I? Mike would kill me if he heard me talking like this."

Harry looked at her.

"Hey, don't get me wrong," Linda protested when she saw the look on Harry's face. "It was just a figure of speech. Mike would never do something like that."

Harry continued to look at her, realizing how effective a good stare could be in forcing people to open up.

"He's a minister, Harriet! He would never kill anyone!" Linda protested.

"Not even a man you were sleeping with?" Harry asked softly.

"Of course not," Linda responded firmly. "Besides, I'm positive he doesn't know about it. Oh, he probably suspects that I've not been faithful down through the years, but he isn't aware of any of the details. And he certainly couldn't know about Wayne."

"Are you sure?" Harry asked.

"I'm positive. Look, I'm very careful, Harriet. I have to be. Any now, if you'll excuse me, I see that our guide has finally arrived." With that, she left Harry and approached a bearded young man in faded blue jeans and a T-shirt.

Chapter 10

Harry strode down Main Street, not paying attention to what their tour guide was saying. She knew Main Street like the back of her hand, they all did, and it hadn't changed much in the past thirty years. A couple of buildings had burned down, new ones had been built to replace them, and some had been painted a different colour. Some stores had gone out of business only to be replaced by new ones. There was a new pizza joint, a video rental outlet, a different hardware store. Their guide had been assigned to work in Spruce Bay during the summer by the provincial tourism department, and he knew more than any of them had ever known about downtown. After a few long-winded speeches, it became evident to Harry that he was intent on imparting his knowledge to them whether they wanted to hear it or not.

"Whose idea was this?" Vivi grumbled as she fell back to walk with Harry.

"As far as I know, Mike and Betty organized the reunion," Margaret responded.

"So where is everybody?" Vivi said plaintively. "I thought there would be more of us."

"Me too," Harry agreed. There had been twenty-three students in their graduating class; last night, ten of them had attended the barbeque, and several others had joined in this morning. Sandy Burns made one more, but still…

"Gather around, folks," Sandy interrupted their guide in a booming voice. "I want you to meet Constable Roger Dalton of the Spruce Bay RCMP detachment. He's going to be assisting me in this investigation."

Harry thought that Constable Dalton looked too young to have a driver's licence. Small towns and villages and rural municipalities were always assigned RCMP officers straight out of training school. They lacked field experience, they lacked maturity, so all they had to go on was what they had learned in their courses and any natural smarts they brought with them. "Ah, Ms. Hubbley," he said in an overly polite manner as he shook her hand. "I'd like to ask you a few questions, if I may."

"Right now?" Harry asked with dismay.

"Why not?" Sandy said with a detached smile.

"But we're in the middle of the tour," Harry protested.

"It doesn't look to me like you're paying much attention to that fellow from the tourism department," Sandy commented. "And you were the only one to have seen Wayne Williams before the barbecue."

Harry glanced at Linda, who looked ill at ease. Why didn't she tell the police that Wayne had dropped by before anyone else had arrived at the barbecue? Linda didn't have to divulge the whole truth; after all, no one would guess that she and Wayne had been making love, especially when guests were expected momentarily. But Linda remained silent.

"Let's go back to the station, then," Dalton proposed.

"Do we need to be so formal about it? Why don't we just have coffee in the restaurant down the street?" Harry suggested, directing a fraudulent smile at them.

"Sure, why not?" Sandy replied.

"Don't we need to be at the station?"

"Naw - it will save time this way," Sandy said, interrupting the young constable. "We'll want to talk to some of the others, so this way we can set up shop and pull them in one at a time."

"So much for a quiet, relaxing tour of the town," Vivi muttered under her breath.

"I wouldn't have minded seeing the school again," Harry said as she walked down Main Street between the two police officers, feeling as if she were under arrest. What was it about cops that made her go all defensive before she was even questioned? She had nothing to hide. She hadn't seen Wayne since they graduated from high school, and their drive from Halifax had been less than illuminating. He had bored her, annoyed her and mystified her, and during the barbecue he had made a nasty insinuation about her sexual orientation before he had disappeared to meet his death.

There was an empty table at the back of the restaurant. Harry realized that she was very hungry and ordered a café-au-lait, scrambled eggs, and a sweet roll. She had missed dinner the night before, and she hadn't had breakfast this morning.

"Lovely weather," Sandy said absently as the waitress served them.

"Yes, we've been lucky," Harry replied, watching the constable fidget. "It could have rained all weekend."

"It's supposed to rain tomorrow," Dalton said as he poured cream into his coffee cup.

Give me a break, Harry thought; didn't they teach him how to make decent conversation?

"We'd like you to go over what you and Wayne Williams talked about when you drove down from Halifax yesterday," Sandy requested once the waitress had placed Harry's plate of scrambled eggs and the sweet roll in front of her.

"But I already told you about that last night."

"I know, but we want to hear about it again," Sandy said.

Harry stifled a sigh and did as he asked, breaking her roll in two and buttering it as she talked.

"It's a long drive and you hadn't seen him in thirty years. Was that all you had to say to each other?" Dalton asked suspiciously.

"I told you, he slept most of the way," Harry replied, biting into her roll and then eating some of the scrambled eggs.

"It's strange that he was so tired in the middle of the day," Dalton insinuated.

"Is it?" Harry retorted curtly. "If you don't believe me, why don't you just say so?"

"I never said I didn't believe you," Dalton protested, turning to Sandy for support.

"Now, Harriet, don't get your dander up," Sandy said in a placatively. "Dalton here doesn't mean anything by it. He's just trying to find out what went on."

"That's right," Dalton said eagerly.

"Did Wayne say that he was going to get in touch with his parents?" Sandy asked.

"No, just the opposite, in fact. He said they didn't get along and that he hadn't told them he was coming," Harry replied, thinking of Wayne's family for the first time. He had been an only child, hadn't he? His parents would be in shock. "Have his parents been told?"

"Yes," Sandy said gruffly. "I went out to their place last night. They live on a farm outside town. Moved there after Wayne finished high school. His old man said taxes were too high in Spruce Bay."

"Are they all right?" Harry asked.

Sandy Burns frowned at her. "What do you think?"

Harry stared at him until he looked away, and then she finished the eggs and roll.

"His mother said she wouldn't mind talking to one of you," Sandy added. "She'd like to know what he'd been up to the past few years."

"I think that will have to wait until we find out who murdered him," Dalton interjected.

"Yes, we wouldn't want the murderer paying a friendly visit to the victim's home, would we?" Harry said sarcastically.

"I hear that Wayne accused you of something last night at the barbecue," Sandy said abruptly.

Who on earth had dredged that up? She had been talking with Linda, Vivi, Betty and Dan when Wayne crept up behind them and insinuated that men were scarce in her life. She had been exasperated, not so much about what he had said, but by the tone in which he had said it. It had been a momentary annoyance about a typical "Wayne" remark. He had always been skulking around the school, listening to private conversations and then tossing off a comment meant to cut to the quick.

"Oh, that," she said with a dismissive laugh. Did they really think that she would kill someone for implying that she was gay?

The two police officers looked at each other and then back at her.

"What did he say to you?" Dalton finally asked.

"That my retention of youthfulness must be due to the scarcity of men in my life," Harry replied when she realized that they were serious.

"What the hell…?" Sandy Burns muttered.

"But that's not much of an insult, is it?" Harry said, sipping her café-au-lait. "And it's certainly not a reasonable motive for murder, especially when pretty well everyone knows that I'm a lesbian."

Dalton choked on his coffee.

Harry ignored his coughing and raised her eyebrows at Sandy Burns, who was occupied in a futile attempt to control the look on his face.

"It's the truth," Harry said. "You can ask the others. I'm sure they'll tell you that they know."

"Fine," Dalton sputtered. "I'll be sure to ask."

"Go get another one of them, Dalton," Sandy said, not taking his eyes from Harry's face.

Dalton looked like he was going to object to doing escort duty but reconsidered when Sandy shot him a look of sheer disgust.

"Sure, Chief," Dalton said. "Which one do you want?"

"I don't care," Sandy sighed. "No, wait. Bring me Vivi Andrews."

Dalton nodded and left the deli.

"Would you like another coffee, Chief Burns?" the waitress asked.

"You bet," he replied emphatically. As soon as the waitress left, he said, 'Tell me, Harriet, did you know you were that way when you and I were going out together?" he asked softly after the waitress had refilled his coffee cup.

Oh, lord, thought Harry with dismay. How could she have forgotten that she had dated Sandy Burns? Memories suddenly flooded back, recollections of fending him off in the back seat of his father's car, of his increasingly serious sexual demands, of lying about why she was breaking up with him when she couldn't tolerate it any longer.

"I should have known there was something wrong with you," he whispered violently. "And you're not even ashamed of it."

"I would never be ashamed about who I am," Harry said with quiet dignity. "Or deny it, either. You're the one who should be ashamed for being so prejudiced."

"Don't give me that crap," he said with a shake of his head.

"Never mind," Harry said as she stood up and tossed some bills on the table. "I didn't expect you to understand." Chief of Police or not, she certainly didn't have to sit there with him for one second longer.

"Just don't forget what I told you before," Sandy said.

"And what might that be," she asked, her voice tight.

"Don't leave town until further notice," he replied with a cold smile.

"Do you think you can keep us here forever?" she asked.

"It's pretty clear that one of you killed him," Sandy replied.

"That may be so, but just don't forget that you're one of us," Harry said as she turned and left the restaurant.

She crossed the street and walked past the post office to her rental car, got in and drove off. How dare he, she fumed.

When the tires squealed around a blind corner, she abruptly removed her foot from the gas pedal and braked. It would do no good to wrap herself around a telephone pole or crash between the bay windows of somebody's house just because she was angry with Sandy. She drove slowly the rest of the way to the Barnacle Motel and pulled info the deserted parking lot.

"Do you have an empty room?" she asked the middle-aged woman in the office. The counter was cluttered with bric-a-brac – dozens of ceramic animals, tiny wood ducks, miniature dolls, Lilliputian lobsters, brightly painted miniature red dories.

"Yeah, we've got a couple left," the woman answered, opening the registration book. "How long are you planning to stay?" she asked, returning Harry's credit card to her.

"I'm not certain," Harry replied as she signed in. "A couple of days, at least."

Harry took the key from her and left the office. She parked the rental car in front of unit nine, retrieved her suitcase from the trunk, opened the door and went in. She turned on the air conditioning unit to disperse the hot, humid and slightly musty air, tossed her suitcase on one of the beds, and flopped dejectedly on the other.

She was so lonely. She missed Judy, but that wasn't the only reason she felt that way. It was the horrid isolation she had always experienced in Spruce Bay. This feeling had been somewhat alleviated when her parents had still lived here, but even then, she had suffered from a certain dislocation. She had always been the returning daughter, no longer child but not yet adult because she hadn't snared a husband and produced children. She was remembered for who she had been rather than for what she had become after she moved away. Her parents had sympathized, but they didn't completely understand. They liked Judy, but they couldn't see her as Harry's spouse. She was Harry's "friend," which was desexualized at best and a denial of the seriousness of her relationship at worst.

"Stop being such a glutton for punishment," Harry muttered to herself, removing her sandals and rolling over. At least she was alive and kicking, not dead like Wayne Williams. Who had killed him? She had pried all morning, and the only result was that she was more confused than when the day started. Vivi likely suspected her of being dishonest, Linda was annoyed, and Sandy Burns had resurrected some ancient memories and was now feeling antagonistic toward her. At this rate, none of her classmates would be speaking to her by the end of the reunion.

Oh, lord. She wished she was home and lying on top of the bed with Judy on a lazy Saturday afternoon on a holiday weekend, revelling in the feel of Judy's skin against hers, her mind filled with the exquisite thought that she didn't have to teach school for two whole months. But she was in Spruce Bay, mixed up in a murder investigation, and Judy was in Montreal with Sarah. Perhaps they were lying on the bed, revelling in the feel of each other's skin… She rubbed her cheek against the rough bedspread and groaned.

Any one of her classmates could have killed Wayne. They all had opportunity, and the more she wormed her way into their personal affairs, the more apparent it became that they all had motives. Wayne had been a busy man; he had remained in touch with everyone. Or nearly everyone, Harry amended, for she had never heard from him.

Vivi probably had the most contact with Wayne after they graduated from high school, and Linda had claimed that Vivi and Wayne had been lovers, an assertion which Harry had no reason to doubt. Harry wondered how far Vivi would go to avoid upsetting that rather sensitive husband of hers. Perhaps she had killed Wayne because she was afraid that her husband would find out about her affair and file for divorce.

Linda's case seemed clearer. She was married to a man who had received some sort of divine revelation in adulthood, which had led him to completely change his life. And Wayne could have threatened Linda that he would tell Mike about their affair. It was completely in character. Wayne would think he was being playful, while Linda would believe that he was threatening her. Could she have killed him to keep him quiet?

Conversely, Mike could have killed Wayne because he was sleeping with Linda. The question was whether he knew about their affair and, if he did, whether he cared if Linda kept it quiet. Linda had said that Mike didn't know about Wayne, but Harry wasn't sure she believed her.

Harry got up, went into the bathroom and splashed cold water on her face. This was stupid. She didn't know enough, not nearly enough. She couldn't retrace everyone's steps during the barbecue, and she was sure the police wouldn't be able to either. There had been ten of them, they had all been drinking to one extent or another, and they had spent most of the evening

running back and forth from the beach to the house to the patio.
Some of them would lie about what they had been doing – the
murderer for certain, but others as well. They would deny talking
to people they had flirted with, they would misjudge how long
they had spent in one place or another, they would lie about how
much they had had to drink, and so on. The police would
certainly ask, and she would inquire about their movements last
evening as well, but likely to no avail.

And what about Betty and Dan and Margaret and Eddie?
What were their motives? And then there was Sandy Burns, not
to mention the classmates she hadn't seem yet. Some detective
she was, she thought, feeling exasperated with herself. She was
drowning in clues, but she had no real evidence of guilt. Or,
unfortunately, of innocence. The only thing she knew was that
she hadn't murdered Wayne.

She stripped, letting her clothes fall to the bathroom
floor, and took a long shower. The hot water rinsed the tension
from her back and shoulders. She washed her short hair until it
squeaked, and then stood under the water for a while longer. She
towelled herself dry, parted her hair with a comb, and rubbed
herself down with lotion. She scooped her clothes from the floor
and left the bathroom. She was tired and confused, and that bed,
narrow as it was, looked awfully inviting.

The afternoon's softball game had been cancelled and
nothing had been scheduled to replace it. She could take a nap
without missing anything and be fresh for the dinner and dance
at the yacht club tonight. Harry drew the curtains and dropped
the bundle of clothes on a chair. She slid between the sheets,
closed her eyes, and was asleep in seconds.

Chapter 11

"So, Eddie, tell me about the real estate business," Harry asked, smiling at the plump, perspiring man sitting across the table from her, hoping he couldn't tell that her smile wasn't entirely genuine. The three-piece rock band began playing an old jive from the 1950s, but no one got up to dance.

Eddie started to take off his sports jacket, and then paused. "Do you mind?" he asked Harry and Margaret.

"Not at all," Harry replied. Anything to stop the sweat from running down his face. It was not an attractive sight.

It had grown hot and humid while she napped, and even though the men had dressed in light summer suits and the women in skimpy dresses, everyone had wilted before cocktail hour was over. Harry had donned her fanciest outfit, a grey silk slit skirt with a matching blouse and high-heeled sandals. She had decided to go without panty hose. It was simply too hot to stand on ceremony.

"The real estate business definitely has its ups and downs," Eddie declared. "You've got to have excellent nerves to stay in this occupation year after year. The only sure thing is that everybody wants a deal. The seller wants to make a bundle, the purchasers want to save a bundle, and nobody wants to pay the agent a plugged nickel."

"Sounds rough," Harry commented, taking a sip of white wine. She put her glass down and slid it away from her. She had already finished a rum and Coke and most of a glass of wine, and she was beginning to feel lightheaded. She filled her water glass and drained it just as the band broke into an idiosyncratic rendition of *Blue Suede Shoes*. It wouldn't have been half bad if the singer knew how to sing.

"Oh, I manage to make a living, but it's certainly not easy," he said.

"You know, it's great to have the opportunity to catch up with everyone," Harry said, loathing the way she sounded. But it was for a good cause, she rationalized. She had to learn more about these people, and the only way to do that was to be friendly and ingratiating and to throw compliments about like there was no tomorrow, even if it made her feel somewhat nauseous. "An ambitious man like you must have had a lot of eligible women buzzing around you. Did you never marry?"

He glanced at Margaret and then smiled wanly. "No, I'm afraid I never did. My dad died shortly after I graduated from high school, and a couple of years later my mother suffered from a series of strokes that left her an invalid. I stayed at home to look after her. She needs round-the-clock care, so I have someone come in while I'm at work."

"Eddie's such a good son," Margaret said with studied sincerity, leaning toward Harry. "He would never consider putting her in a nursing home."

Harry bet that Margaret had thought of that option, and often. Who could blame her?

"Meanwhile, Margaret and I are dating," Eddie said cheerfully.

"Actually, we've been engaged since last Christmas," Margaret said, showing Harry a diamond which was brighter than her smile.

"You could get married and still take care of your mother," Harry suggested.

"Oh, Mother wouldn't like that," Eddie told her firmly.

"I see," Harry answered. Had Margaret waited for over thirty years? Was that a Beatles tune the band was trying to play? She turned and watched Linda and Mike do an expert jive and felt envious; she and Judy had never jived successfully because they both wanted to lead. It was a bone of contention in their dancing relationship, one which they took quite seriously.

"I have my work, too," Margaret said swiftly. "I'm an accountant with the regional hospital."

"Oh, so you went away to study," Harry said.

"Yes, to Halifax," Margaret replied, her earnest expression lightening. "I took my accounting degree at Dalhousie University, and then I worked for a large firm in Halifax for several years. I came home to visit my parents nearly every weekend, and that's when Eddie and I started going together. Then my mother died, and a year later, my father passed on. Shortly after that, I decided to move back home and live in the house myself. It was either that or sell it or rent it out, neither of which I wanted to do. An accountant can find work almost anywhere, you know."

"And you're still living there," Harry said.

"Yes," Margaret confirmed.

"Did you ever see Wayne Williams when he came home to visit?" Harry asked.

"Heavens, no!" Margaret exclaimed with a laugh, the first genuine one Harry had heard from her all weekend. "Oh, I might have passed him on Main Street, but we would say hello and that would be it. He wasn't our type of person."

"What Margie means, Harriet, is that Wayne was a little too wild for us," Eddie explained solemnly. "He was that way in high school and from what I heard, he was as bad, if not worse, once he went away."

"Of course, we both know that times have changed," Margaret said.

"And just because we decided to wait until we got married doesn't mean that other people have to do the same thing," Eddie added.

Did he mean that they were both still virgins? It couldn't be, Harry thought, waving at Betty and Dan as they entered the club.

"We don't have anything against couples who don't wait until they're married," Margaret explained. "Or against couples who live together without being married."

It was true, then; they *were* virgins!

"Remember when we were young, Harriet?" Margaret asked suddenly.

"I certainly do," Harry said, her throat constricting. Hell, they weren't *that* old – but Eddie and Margaret sounded like octogenarians who had been put out to pasture decades before!

"Well, back then it was a scandal to be sexually active," Margaret continued, encouraged by Harry's affirmation. "Look at how we shunned girls who went all the way, for example."

Harry nodded although she had never shunned anyone; actually, it was just as well that they hadn't remembered.

"What Margie means is that we realize things aren't the same today, so we've had to come to some sort of accommodation, or we wouldn't have any friends left," Eddie said with a smile.

It was only when Margaret burst into laughter that Harry realized that Eddie had made a joke. She managed a chuckle to indicate that she had understood his intent.

"Actually, we're quite broadminded these days," he added. "We don't even mind about you."

"How kind," Harry found herself responding, which made her drain her wine glass in shock.

"Have another," Eddie suggested, filling her glass from the bottle on the table.

"But we do have to draw the line somewhere, don't we?" Margaret said rhetorically.

Harry didn't see why, but she didn't mention it.

"So, we no longer frown on serious relationships outside of marriage," Eddie continued. "I hope, by the way, that you are in a serious relationship," he added, pausing for Harry's response.

"Eleven years," Harry muttered, momentarily resisting the urge to get up and run. Was sitting through a conversation like this an integral part of being a detective? If so, she was going to resign at the first opportunity.

Eddie and Margaret nodded sagely at each other.

"It's promiscuity that we can't accept," Margaret said decisively.

"And adultery," Eddie added.

"Adultery for certain," Margaret stressed. "All these couples cheating on each other, ruining their relationships over a little bit lust. They've got no self-control, that's what it is. And what happens to the children?"

"In a small town like this, everyone knows what's going on," Eddie told Harry. "It's disgusting how much adultery there is."

"Anyone I know?" Harry asked impulsively. Lord, she was just as revolting as they were. But she was doing her job. She didn't really suspect either of them of having murdered Wayne, but she had to find out, as discreetly and efficiently as possible, if they knew anything about the others.

Eddie and Margaret glanced at each other and then at Harry.

"I can keep a secret," Harry added encouragingly.

"Gosh, there's been so much going on that I don't know where to start," Margaret replied.

Not with Sodom and Gomorrah, Harry prayed irreverently. She couldn't wait that long. "If it's a bother, we don't have to get into it right now."

"Oh, it's no bother at all," Margaret hastened to say.

Harry had been right; Margaret was bursting to gossip.

"I think I'll visit the little boy's room," Eddie said, rising from the table. "This is girls' talk, so you'll probably feel more comfortable without me."

"Fine, fine," Harry said. The band had stopped playing, ending its first set with a ragged and off-key rendition of Patsy Cline's *Crazy*. Where did a man get off trying to sing that song, Harry wondered.

"Give us a few minutes, dear," Margaret said sweetly.

"Right," he said with a stolid smile. Harry watched him shove his hands in his pants pockets and walk toward the washrooms.

"Harriet, sometimes I think that you and I are the only two girls in our class who didn't sleep with Wayne Williams," Margaret said as soon as Eddie was out of earshot.

"You're kidding!" Harry exclaimed involuntarily.

"Not in the least," Margaret replied. "I know for a fact that at one time or another, he slept with Vivi, Linda and Betty, not to mention Sandy Burns' wife and some others who haven't come to the reunion."

"I knew about Vivi and Linda," Harry said, moving her chair closer to Margaret's. "But Betty? And Sandy Burns' wife – what was her name?"

"Julia," Margaret reminded her. "She was two years younger, that's probably why you don't remember her. She and Wayne had this torrid affair when we were in grade twelve and she was in grade ten. That was before Sandy started going with her. I believe she was on the rebound from Wayne when Sandy asked her out. Eventually, they ended up getting married."

"Did Sandy know about Wayne?" Harry asked.

"I don't know for sure, but I don't see why not. Everyone else did," Margaret replied. "Julia and Wayne weren't particularly secretive about their relationship. They came to school dances together. In fact, they went everywhere together. I can remember how disgusting I thought they were, kissing and touching each other in public like they did. Even then it was clear to me that they were sexually intimate. He acted like he owned her body," she said with a nervous laugh, as if the memory might contaminate her.

"Then Sandy must have known," Harry mused.

"Unless he was living in a different world," Margaret answered with more wryness than Harry had credited her with having.

Sandy wasn't overly bright; could he have been so obtuse that he hadn't noticed his future wife's relationship with Wayne? She tried to recall what kind of reputation Julia had, but her mind was a blank. She couldn't remember the younger girl at all. "What was Julia like?" she asked Margaret.

"She was a giggler, Margaret replied. "That's all I remember about her. Every time one of the boys said something, she giggled whether it was funny or not."

One of those, Harry thought with dismay. No one would ever discover what she was really like because her lips were too busy smiling to say much of anything. "Did she run with one of the wild crowds?"

"No, I don't think so," Margaret said. "I believe Wayne was her first serious relationship. After that, she went straight to Sandy."

It was clear as mud. Sandy Burns doubtlessly knew that his wife had been Wayne's lover. Then again, maybe he didn't. If he knew, he either accepted it or he didn't, which probably depended on when he found out about it. If he had known when they were in high school, he had evidently not cared. And if he found out after they were married, he probably wouldn't have minded. It would have been ancient history. Besides, if Sandy had wanted revenge, why would he have waited for such a long time? It didn't make any sense. And Julia had left him, not the other way around. Anyway, Harry thought that Wayne had likely been killed for something more recent than helping Julia lose her virginity all those years ago.

"And then there was Vivi, who would sleep with anyone with pants on," Margaret said rancorously. "I'm sorry to have to say that about her, but it's true."

Harry could tell just how sorry Margaret was, which was hardly at all. But she didn't say a thing to defend Vivi. Besides, she knew that Margaret was right.

"She hated me, you know."

"No, I didn't know," Harry responded, trying to remember whether Vivi had ever mentioned Margaret, who had been one of those colorless classmates who never did anything notable or said anything clever or made any real impression.

"She thought I was after Wayne, but she couldn't have been more mistaken," Margaret said prudishly.

"Why on earth would she think that?" Harry asked, her attention piqued.

"I have no idea," Margaret responded. "Although you know how possessive some girls get about their boyfriends. To ward me off, she told me that she was having sexual relations with him, although those were not the precise words she used."

Harry suppressed a grin because she could all too easily imagine what Vivi had said. "What I find hard to believe is that Betty ever had an affair with Wayne," Harry commented. "There was never any gossip about them, either. If I remember rightly, she and Dan started going out in grade nine, and that was that."

"Oh, but that's not true," Margaret said. "I know they went steady all through high school, but my family's house was right behind Betty's, and I saw Wayne Williams sneak in the back door of her house more than once."

"But that doesn't prove anything," Harry protested. "He could have been going over to her house to study, or something."

"Don't be silly – do you ever remember Wayne studying?" Margaret said with a laugh. "Besides, every time he paid her a visit, her parent's car was gone. So don't tell me they were sitting there staring at a book, Harriet Hubbley."

This was mind-boggling. "What grade were we in?" Harry asked.

"Twelve," Margaret responded.

"And how often did it happen?"

"Often enough," Margaret said. "Don't forget that I wasn't always able to notice him coming or going. And go he did. He invariably scooted out of there before her parents got home. I don't think that anyone knew about their affair except the two of them. And me, of course, but I never let on. The only person I ever told before tonight was Eddie. Eventually Wayne stopped coming around. And after we graduated Betty went off to Halifax to take a secretarial course. She came back the next year and took a position in an office."

"How long was it before she and Dan got married?" Harry asked.

"I don't really remember," Margaret said. "It didn't take long for Dan to be hired on one of the boats, so they likely got married pretty soon after that."

"Wayne and Betty! I just don't believe it!" Harry said, shaking her head in amazement.

"Quite a little devil with the ladies, wasn't he?" Margaret commented.

"Quite," Harry agreed as Eddie returned to the table.

"Have another glass of wine," Eddie suggested.

"I think I'd better have something to eat first," Harry replied. "It's been nice talking with you."

They beamed. Harry smiled back, got up and walked across the room.

Chapter 12

"Where have you been?" Harry asked Vivi as she passed her table. She hadn't seen her come in.

"Oh, I couldn't decide what to wear," Vivi replied nonchalantly. "Why don't you join me? I *hate* sitting alone."

"I'm in need of some nourishment," Harry responded, pointing toward the buffet table. "But I'll be right back."

The band was playing a simply dreadful interpretation of a Paul Anka ballad. As she helped herself to a spoonful of watery potato salad, several dry-looking sandwiches, some pieces of salami and sliced chicken and a couple of pickles, she contemplated which was flatter – the saxophone or the singer. It was truly awful, but no one else seemed to notice. Betty and Dan and Mike and Linda were among the couples on the dance floor.

"Dale and Ethel," she said cheerfully as she passed a waltzing couple. "Nice to see you again."

Nods and smiles, nods and smiles, she thought tiredly as she approached the bar. She was thankful that she recognized most of them, although it was startling how much weight Bobby Jones had lost. He had been such a chubby boy in school, and now he was so skinny!

"Let me guess," the bartender said with a wide smile. "A glass of white wine for the little lady."

"Make it a bottle," Harry sighed.

"It's your hangover," the bartender shrugged as he popped the cork.

"Thanks," Harry responded, carrying her plate and the bottle back to Vivi's table.

"So here I am, still alone," Vivi complained. "Thank God you brought more wine. You know, they avoid single women like the plague in this hick town."

"Really?" Harry sat down and started to eat. She cut off a piece of salami, forked it to her mouth and then grimaced. It was so salty that she couldn't swallow it. She raised her napkin and spat the meat into it, then folded the napkin and placed it on her plate.

"You can't eat it either," Vivi remarked with a laugh. "Do you believe this set-up? A lousy band and food from hell."

"Where is everybody?" Harry asked, pouring herself a glass of wine. Vivi's table was littered with empty plates, wine glasses, beer bottles and smelly ashtrays. The band was playing a puzzling rendition of a Neil Sedaka tune which had been on top of the pop charts in the early 1960s. "It looks like you had a full table at one time this evening."

"I don't know where they went," Vivi responded, "And I don't care. I was the lucky recipient of a visit from our illustrious Police Chief and his young but trusty RCMP companion the second I walked in. Roy Rodgers and Trigger, although I bet Trigger was more intelligent. Why would they decide to interrogate me here? And such questions! I lied, of course. Any self-respecting suspect would."

"Sandy Burns has no sense," Harry responded, remembering her interview with the two policemen.

"How right you are," Vivi said. "I suppose I shouldn't have lied, though."

"What did you lie about?" Harry asked.

"Pretty darn near everything," Vivi answered smugly. "It seems they were looking for me earlier today when they finished with you, but they couldn't find me."

"Where'd you go?" Harry asked casually, refilling Vivi's wine glass. She would have to stop drinking soon or leave her rental car at the yacht club and hitch a ride home with someone else.

"Oh, I happened to run into Leslie Rossiter during the tour. Remember him?" Vivi asked.

"Of course – he was the principal's son," Harry said immediately. "Everyone always said that his father made sure he got good grades."

"Well, he showed up when the tour of Main Street was nearly over, and we hit it off right away," Vivi said. "I admit that he was a bit of a dolt in high school, but he's grown into a good-looking and rather interesting man. He runs a small engineering firm in Halifax and seems to be doing well. He invited me for lunch, and since I wasn't particularly interested in seeing the school, I accepted."

"Of course," Harry replied with a smile.

"Don't look at me like that, Harriet Hubbley; it was just for lunch," Vivi protested. "We drove down to Chester and ate in one of those trendy new restaurants and then drove straight back here."

"And what did you have for dessert?" Harry asked with a grin.

"Not each other, if that's what you mean," Vivi retorted instantly. "Not that I would have minded, but he didn't ask. It was all very polite, civilized and above-board. Unfortunately."

"You ought to be more careful," Harry said in a more serious tone.

"Don't worry about me, I'm as careful as I need to be," Vivi replied lightly.

"Is Leslie coming tonight?" Harry asked, looking around. The yacht looked cavernous with just their small group in it, and she wondered why they hadn't rented the smaller Legion Hall or one of the church halls. There couldn't have been more then forty of them spread among several tables, and the yacht club could hold two hundred.

"Oh, he's over there with his wife," Vivi answered, pointing to a table across the room.

She shouldn't have been surprised that Leslie was married, Harry realized. Had Vivi wanted Leslie, the existence of a wife wouldn't have made a bit of difference. "I suppose I should go over and say hello," Harry said with a notable lack of enthusiasm.

"Don't bother if you don't want to," Vivi responded, retrieving a lone pickle from one of the plates and biting off half of it. "I'm dying for something good to eat," she moaned.

"It would be funny to come back here for our reunion and end up not speaking to some of our classmates, wouldn't it?" Harry commented, watching Leslie Rossiter chat animatedly with the others at his table. He hadn't changed much. His black hair was still short, although it was longer than the brush cut which had topped his head in high school, even after the Beatles had made long hair fashionable on boys. The only notable difference was that he had gained weight, and his once thin, big-boned frame was now filled out.

"Which one is his wife?" she asked Vivi.

"The one to his left, I believe," Vivi answered. "I don't know her name, but I heard he married a girl from Church Pond. Do you recognize anyone else at that table?"

Harry looked at the other couple. The rather corpulent woman looked familiar, but not the man. "No, but I suppose I should."

"That's Patsy Burns," Vivi announced. "You know, Sandy Burns' twin sister. She married some fellow from the Annapolis Valley."

"That's Patsy Burns? You've got to be kidding!" Harry responded.

"No, I'm not," Vivi replied. "I couldn't believe it either. Do you remember how skinny she used to be?"

"It's been a long time since we graduated, Vivi," Harry said, sighing.

"Don't remind me," Vivi said with a shiver. "Whenever I think about that, I feel someone walking on my grave."

"Don't be macabre," Harry scolded her, taking a sip of wine.

"Wayne is the first of us to die," Vivi said sadly. "It's the beginning of the end."

"You've had too much wine," Harry said somewhat harshly. She avoided being drawn into discussions about death whenever she could. She didn't believe in the existence of any god, and she had no opinion about life after death, so she disliked talking about it. How ironic, then, that she was trying to solve Wayne's murder.

"So have you," Vivi laughed. "Let's go back to your motel room and make love."

"Shhh!" Harry told her. "You don't have to invite everyone!"

"Nobody's paying any attention to us," Vivi laughed reassuringly. Then she gave Harry a knowing look. "But you don't want to make love with me again, do you?"

Harry was such a coward when difficulties arose in her relationships. Judy said she would be better off telling the truth right from the beginning, no matter how much it hurt. And Judy grew frustrated with Harry when she deferred to someone else's wishes and did things she didn't want to because she was reluctant to say no. This tendency came from having been taught to be selfless when she was growing up. She had only learned later that this attribute often placed her at a disadvantage. Unfortunately, it would likely take her the rest of her life to rid herself of this pernicious habit.

"You don't care for me, do you?" Vivi asked sadly.

"I just don't think it would work, Vivi," Harry replied, emptying the last of the wine into their glasses. The members of the band were returning to the stage and picking up their instruments. "When we were in high school, I loved you so much that I thought I was going to die. But things change."

"You changed."

"I grew up," Harry clarified, "and learned to stop banging my head against a wall."

"Meaning?"

"I quit chasing straight women," Harry said with a grin.

Vivi reached under the table and slid her hand up Harry's thigh.

"Don't," Harry said even though Vivi's touch aroused her. It would be easy to give in, to drive back to the motel and make love late into the night. Thirty years ago, when they were in school, she would have thought she had died and gone to heaven if Vivi had touched her as intimately as this.

The hand withdrew.

"Thank you," Harry murmured.

"Don't think I didn't know how you felt about me," Vivi said. "And you know, you tempted me. You wanted me so bad I could feel it."

"*Feel* it? Hell, I could *taste* it," Harry said in a droll voice.

Vivi laughed. "That's quite a compliment."

"I meant it as such," Harry said gently.

"But back then I thought it had to be one thing or the other, either boys or girls, and you know what people said about doing it with girls," Vivi remarked.

"Some people still do," Harry replied dryly.

Vivi snorted and finished her glass of wine. "I was crazy about sex," she confided. "I couldn't get enough of it. I tried to be reasonable in high school, but even so, I managed to acquire quite a reputation. It was much better when I moved to Toronto. I could do what I wanted to, although I found I had to be careful. Some of the men I met were dangerous. I was surprised to discover that a lot of what they say about big cities is true. I finally got married because I met someone who was sexually compatible, but it didn't take me long to realize that there's more to a long-term relationship than sex. Isn't that a bore?" she asked Harry, and then continued without waiting for an answer. "My second husband rarely wants sex, so I carry on very quiet affairs. You're the first woman I've ever made love with. Do you think there's more wine?"

What? The first woman? Harry's mouth suddenly went dry.

"We're being too anti-social. Let's go see if anybody else has some wine," Vivi suggested, rising from her chair.

"Are you okay?" Harry asked, standing up so abruptly that her chair threatened to fall over backwards. She didn't notice.

"Oh, hell, yes," Vivi said with a toss of her head. "You were wonderful. And I feel fine."

"I didn't know," Harry said apologetically. "I thought that you must…"

"Be bisexual?" Vivi finished for her.

Harry nodded.

"Not really," Vivi replied. "But when I saw you again after all those years, when I realized that you were still attracted to me, I decided to take the initiative."

"You certainly did," Harry said. But she wasn't all that attracted to Vivi. Not really. Certainly not the way she had been in high school.

"Of course," Vivi said with the hint of a smile. "You never knew how tempted I was when we were in high school. You thought the attraction was one-sided, but you were wrong. Maybe I was scared to act on my feelings, or maybe I was just too busy with the boys. When I saw that the old magnetism was still there, my first reaction was to ignore it. Then I reconsidered. I haven't had many women friends in my life – a lot of women find me threatening. But I remembered how you always liked me, no matter how awful I acted toward you. So, I decided to find out what it was like."

"And?" Harry asked. If they moved any closer to each other, Sandy Burns would have reason to cross the room and arrest them. She resisted the urge to reach out and touch Vivi and forced herself to take a step backwards.

"I really enjoyed it," Vivi replied.

Enjoyed? Boy, she had sure set herself up for that one, Harry thought dismally.

"That wasn't the right thing to say, I take it," Vivi said, looking amused.

"Let's go find some more wine," Harry said impotently, turning away before Vivi could laugh at her. Friendly fire or not, she didn't want to be on the receiving end of it.

Chapter 13

The doorbell was ringing. Harry sat up swiftly and then grasped her head between her hands. Lord, she had a bad headache! How much had she had to drink after she and Vivi had joined Betty and Dan Richards and Mike and Linda Schmidt? Thank goodness Eddie had been sober and had offered to drive her back to the motel. She had abandoned her rental car at the yacht club, but she was certain she could find someone to drive her back there after the church service tomorrow morning so she could pick it up.

The doorbell rang again. Why was someone intent on visiting her in the middle of the night? Couldn't they tell by now that she wasn't going to open the door? She groaned and fumbled for the switch on the base of the lamp sitting on the bedside table. By the time she succeeded in turning it on, she was awake enough to realize that it was not quite one in the morning and that it was the telephone and not the doorbell that was ringing.

"Hello?" she said, wishing she had a glass of water. Her mouth was dry and tasted like a stale ashtray.

"Hi babe!"

"Judy?" Harry exclaimed, her heartbeat increasing. "What's wrong?"

"Nothing's wrong, silly. I'm just worried about you," Judy replied. "I heard on the news that someone was murdered in Spruce Bay, but there weren't many details. Are you all right?"

"I'm hung-over, if you really want to know," Harry replied. "Other than that, I'm fine."

"You know you shouldn't drink so much around all those straight people," Judy scolded. "But what happened? Who was murdered?"

Harry told her as briefly as possible.

"I don't like it, Harry," Judy said, her voice alarmed. "It sounds like nearly any one of them could have killed him, from your nutty fundamentalist friend to your old flame."

"Well, unlike you city slickers who had new classmates every year, I spent twelve years with this bunch, so there are bound to be complications," Harry explained, ignoring the

question Judy had tacitly raised by using the term "old flame."
"You might say that some of us know each other too well."

"It must be confusing to see them again with so many
years of life in between," Judy remarked. "Am I to presume by
your avoidance of the topic that your old flame has become your
renewed flame?"

"It's almost like coming back in another incarnation, if
you know what I mean. People are the same and yet different,"
Harry replied, wishing she hadn't had so much to drink. It made
it difficult to think of how best to deal with telling Judy about
Vivi. Still, Judy was having a long-term affair with Sarah, so
why did Harry feel so guilty about Vivi?

"So how was she?" Judy asked. "What was her name
again? Suzy-Q? Barbie?"

Harry laughed despite herself, although she could hear
the slight stiffness in her lover's voice. But Judy had
relinquished the right to feel jealous when she'd taken a lover.
Right? "Vivi."

"Short for Vivian?"

"Short for Bridget."

"Go figure," Judy said dryly.

"I'm sorry," Harry said. She didn't know why she felt
guilty about making love with Vivi when Judy was involved in
an on-going relationship with Sarah, but there it was. As Judy
said, go figure.

"If you apologize one more time, I'll hang up on you,"
Judy said, her voice tight with anger.

"I made a mistake," Harry said quietly.

"So, don't tell me about it," Judy replied calmly.

"No, I want to," Harry hastened to assure her. "It's just
that it really was a mistake. Remember I told you I'd be staying
with my classmates Betty and Dan? Well, what I didn't know
was that Betty had also invited Vivi to stay in the same room. To
make a long story short, we ended up making love last night."

"And it was no good for you?" Judy asked.

"She's straight, Judy," Harry confessed.

"Shit!" Judy exclaimed. "Did you have to? Is she going
out with any men? Were you careful?"

"Yes, yes, and yes. And don't worry, I'm not going to do
it again. I moved out of Betty and Dan's and checked into a
motel this morning," Harry said, not wanting to discuss the finer

details of safer sex, which she could tell Judy was on the verge of doing.

"I know," Judy replied. "I tried to call you there and someone gave me this number."

"I'm glad you called," Harry said. "I miss you." Did Judy miss her, she wondered, or was she so preoccupied with Sarah that she didn't have time to think about Harry?

"I'm worried about you Harry," Judy said. "Are you still coming home on Monday?"

"I'm supposed to, but I'm not sure now," Harry told her, feeling depressed. Judy hadn't said she missed her, so she knew the answer to that question.

"What do you mean?"

"We've been told not to leave town," Harry replied.

"You can't be serious."

"Quite serious," Harry said. "Both the town police force and the RCMP are investigating, and we've been asked to stay here until they find out who did it."

"Do they have any leads?"

"Not as far as I know," Harry sighed. "Look, I went to school with the Chief of Police, and believe me, he's not too bright."

"Oh, great!"

"And the RCMP constable is nearly as bad," Harry complained. "Besides, he's so young."

"Are you saying that you won't be home until Christmas?" Judy said, trying to keep her voice light.

"Possibly Labour Day, Thanksgiving for sure," Harry replied in the same vein.

"Let's get serious," Judy said, clearing her throat. "How much danger are you in?"

"Danger?" Harry echoed her lover's word. "I haven't really thought about it."

"Who do you think killed him?"

"I don't know yet," Harry said, and then she realized that she had fallen into Judy's trap. "That wasn't fair," she complained. "How did you know?"

"I've only lived with you for eleven years," Judy replied dryly. "And it's the same as Cape Cod; you're too curious to leave it alone. When something mysterious is going on, you want to know why. If no one else can find out who murdered him,

you're going to stick your nose it. I just don't want it to get
bloodied. Or worse."

"I'm being cautious," Harry assured her.

"Like a bull in a china shop, right?" Judy remarked.

"I wish you were here," Harry said suddenly.

Dead silence.

"Well, I do," Harry said harshly, irritated about not being
able to say what she wanted to in case it put too many demands
on Judy while she was with Sarah or in case it offended Sarah or
made either Judy or Sarah feel guilty. Judy and Sarah's territory
as a couple had to remain inviolate even though its boundaries
were not easily defined, but Harry didn't feel that there was the
same respect for the boundaries of her relationship with Judy.
Judy said that there were, but Harry just couldn't recognize them
yet. But what about her as an individual? When did her needs get
taken care of? She hated having a third person in the equation.

"I hear you," Judy said calmly. "But I've got to go now."

"Fine."

"I'll call you tomorrow."

"Fine."

"Don't be like this," Judy implored. "It's not good for
you. Or for us."

Not good for us? Which us? Judy and Sarah or Judy and
her? Sarah, probably, Harry thought rebelliously, but she didn't
say anything.

"I can't help it. And you told me not to apologize again,"
Harry replied stonily.

"So I did," Judy said with a sad laugh. "But I will call
you tomorrow. Good night, Harry."

"Good night," Harry whispered. She waited until she
heard the click at the other end of the line and then slowly
replaced the receiver. She felt like crying but resisted the urge.
Her head hurt enough as it was.

She went into the bathroom, splashed cold water on her
face and rubbed it vigorously with a towel. She poured herself a
glass of water and took it back into the bedroom with her.
Turning off the air conditioner, she piled the pillows against the
wall and slid between the sheets. She had been asking questions
all day, but she was not one bit closer to discovering who had
killed Wayne Williams.

Although Wayne had left Spruce Bay after graduation, he had never really abandoned it. He had returned often and had remained in close contact with some of their former classmates. Very close, she mused, thinking of his on-going sexual relationship with Linda. And Vivi, although their affair had unfolded in Toronto, far away from the prying eyes of the gossip mongers in Spruce Bay. But according to Margaret, Wayne and Vivi had first become lovers when they were students in high school. And she couldn't forget Betty, although there was no evidence that she and Wayne had continued their relationship after grade twelve.

Wayne had probably been killed because of something that had happened in Spruce Bay, either in the old days when they had been young or sometime since then. She grinned and took a sip of water; what a fine detective she was. Now all she had to do was trace their movements for the past thirty years! And how many suspects were there? Vivi, Betty and Dan, Linda and Mike. Sandy Burns was an unlikely candidate, but she couldn't count him out. And since they had been at the barbecue the night Wayne was murdered, she couldn't overlook Eddie, Margaret and Teresa. Especially Teresa, whose savage destruction of her glass of rum and Coke had shocked Harry. Whether this violent act signalled that Teresa could kill another human being was another question. She would have to find a reason to chat with Teresa, something she was not looking forward to.

Harry had read somewhere that most murderers were committed because of sex or greed. Well, she didn't have to be a real detective to know that sex was writ large all over this one from start to finish. How had Wayne managed to bed so many women? But perhaps that was the wrong question. She should instead be asking why so many of the women she knew had gone to bed with him, especially when most of them had succumbed to his charms while they were still in high school. She didn't even want to consider the number of women he had slept with since then.

Harry finished her glass of water. Her headache had nearly vanished, and she was beginning to feel human again. It was clear that she wasn't going to discover who had killed him until she knew more about Wayne himself.

Someone knocked on the door.

Harry glanced at the clock radio on the bedside table and wondered who was paying her a visit at nearly two in the morning.

Whoever it was knocked again.

"Harry? Wake up! I've got to talk to you!"

Vivi.

Harry slid out of bed and opened the door. "What are you doing here in the middle of the night? And how did you get here?"

"I walked, silly. It took me about five minutes. Remember, we're not in Toronto or Montreal. As to why I'm here, I couldn't sleep and I was too bored to stay in that damned house one second longer," Vivi replied, tossing her jacket on the chair near the door.

"You decided to leave at two in the morning?" Harry asked dubiously.

"Is it that late? I hadn't noticed. Have you got something to drink?" Vivi asked, looking around.

"Water," Harry replied. "And plenty of it."

"That's not what I mean, and you know it," Vivi retorted. She sat on the edge of the bed, opened her purse and took out a mickey of rum.

"You drink too much," Harry said as Vivi raised the bottle to her lips.

"Ah," Vivi said, wiping her mouth with the back of her hand. "That's better. And don't lecture me. Moderation is not my middle name, as you very well know. Are your sure you won't have some?"

"I already had too much to drink tonight," Harry replied.

"Didn't we all, though?" Vivi laughed. "This reunion is threatening to turn into one hell of a drunken party. Too bad Wayne isn't around to enjoy it."

Harry moved Vivi's jacket and sat on the edge of the chair.

"Why are you sitting so far away from me?" Vivi inquired with an amused look on her face. "Afraid I'll bite?"

"You could say something like that," Harry responded, watching Vivi take another sip of rum from her bottle.

"Why, Harriet, don't you know you can trust me?" Vivi simpered.

"That will be the day," Harry said sarcastically. Honestly, Vivi would have been a natural in the acting profession. Once this was over, Harry made a mental note to ask Vivi why she hadn't persevered.

"We were all pretty spiffed last night," Vivi said, studying rum bottle. It was half-full. Or half-empty, depending on how you looked at it.

"Tell me about it," Harry said with feeling, wondering whether Vivi was going to empty the bottle before dawn and whether she had to sit there and watch her do it. "Perhaps the booze wouldn't have had such an effect on me if the food hadn't been so lousy, but I'll tell you, I woke up about half an hour ago with a doozie of a hangover. Want some water?"

"Sure," Vivi said absently.

Harry picked up her glass and went into the bathroom, filled it, and then filled a second one for Vivi. She glanced swiftly at herself in the mirror and grimaced. Her eyes were red-rimmed and her short, blond hair was flat on one side and sticking up on the other. She ran her fingers through it and succeeded in making it worse. But never mind. She didn't care that she looked like she had just got out of bed after a particularly hard night, especially since it was true.

Like hell, she thought as she handed Vivi a glass of water. Whether Vivi was hetero or not, married or not, Harry would always feel something for her – a slight flutter in the pit of her stomach, an urge to reach out and touch her, an emotional lurch that transported her back in time.

"Thanks," Vivi said, taking a sip of water and then pouring rum into her glass. "Are you sure you won't have some?"

Oh, what the hell, Harry decided. Who was she to criticize Vivi when she hadn't been capable to driving her car back to the motel earlier this evening? She held out her glass and let Vivi top up the water with rum.

"So. Where was I?" Vivi asked. "Well, after Eddie dropped you off, he drove me back to Dan and Betty's. Dan was drunk as a skunk and had apparently already staggered off to bed, but Betty was waiting up for me. Would you believe that she offered me a drink?"

"Which you, of course, refused," Harry joked.

"Of course," Vivi said at once. "We sat and talked while I watched her drink."

Harry laughed at this improbable image.

"And then she had another," Vivi said. "Making up for lost time, I guess. She was sober at the yacht club."

"I believe she was their designated driver."

"It's a good thing there were a few of them around or we'd still be there," Vivi chuckled. "Waiting for Miss Goody Two Shoes to sober up enough to drive her car."

Harry saluted Vivi with her glass and had a sip. "At least I had the sense not to drive."

"Yes, that's true," Vivi agreed. "Not like Mike. I hope the two of them got home okay. It would be quite a scandal if one of the local holy rollers got picked up for drunk driving."

"What did you and Betty talk about?" Harry asked.

"Oh, things," Vivi replied obscurely.

"What sort of things?" Harry pressed, wondering whether Vivi was being vague because she had been too drunk to remember or because she didn't want to tell Harry about it.

"Girl-talk," Vivi grinned. "You know."

It was so easy to be heterosexual, Harry thought, so convenient to assume that everyone around you was on the same wavelength. "You mean men," Harry clarified.

"What did you think I meant?" Vivi asked, raising her eyebrows.

"Oh, the weather, the price of gas, the most recent sightings of unidentified flying objects," Harry replied casually. "Or women. You know."

Vivi looked puzzled for a second and then irritated. "Don't play with me, Harry. Or criticize me."

"Then don't assume we have the same understanding of things," Harry replied quietly.

"I'm not changing my perceptions – or assumptions – about anything if I don't have to," Vivi retorted. "At this point in life, I'd have to have a pretty important reason to bother."

"And you don't consider this to be important?" Harry said.

"I thought that was obvious."

"Is that so," Harry said, feeling like she had been slapped in the face. Lightly, but it was still a slap.

"Yes," Vivi replied. "And don't look at me like that. We made love, not promises."

Harry nodded and took another drink.

"Harriet, don't you dare disillusion me by telling me that you're a romantic," Vivi told her. "I don't think I could stand it."

"Then I won't tell you," Harry said harshly.

"I should have known better," Vivi muttered into her drink. "I kept telling myself, but did I listen? No, of course not."

"This drink is too strong," Harry said abruptly, getting up and walking into the bathroom. So that was what a first-class fool looked like, she thought, staring at herself in the mirror.

"Harriet?"

"Coming." She switched off the light and returned to the bedroom.

"Give me a break, Harriet," Vivi said. "I didn't mean to be so rough on you."

As an apology, that would have to do. "Never mind. It doesn't matter. We're both big girls now," Harry replied, wishing it was true. Whoever Vivi had been, whatever Vivi had become, she was not someone with whom you would trust your soul.

"Sure, sure," Vivi said archly. "You look about ready to graduate from kindergarten."

"Cut it out, Vivi," Harry said harshly, rising from the chair and putting her half-finished drink down on the dresser. The slight burning sensation in her diaphragm signalled that it had been a bad idea to start drinking again. "We shouldn't have made love, so let's just forget it ever happened."

"What?" Vivi said, sounding startled.

"What the hell are you thinking about?"

Vivi started to laugh.

"No, never mind," Harry said. "I take that back. I don't want to know."

"Smart lady," Vivi said, finishing her drink in a business-like fashion. "You know, despite what you said at the yacht club tonight, I thought you still might be interested, but I see I was wrong. Besides, I don't particularly want to be involved with someone who can't take care of herself. So how about removing your suitcase from the other bed so this very weary woman can get some beauty sleep?"

Of course, Harry thought; she should have known it wasn't boredom or insomnia that had motivated Vivi to get up in the middle of the night and walk through the deserted streets to get to the motel. Vivi had wanted to make love again, that was all. And now she had withdrawn the offer. Harry picked up her glass, drained it, and then closed her suitcase and placed it on the floor.

"Thanks," Vivi said with a sigh. She got up and put her empty glass on the dresser.

"Don't mention it," Harry replied curtly, walking into the bathroom.

"No, I mean it," Vivi said. "And don't worry, dear heart, I'll rent my own room in the morning."

But Harry had closed the door behind her and didn't hear what Vivi had said.

Chapter 14

Harry was so thankful that Vivi wasn't there when she woke up that she didn't wonder where she had gone. She showered briskly and rummaged through her suitcase to find something appropriate to wear to the ecumenical church service, trying not to feel depressed. It was a losing battle, however; she was disillusioned about Vivi. It had come on gradually, like some migraine headaches. First there was the tingle of doubt that Vivi was the same girl she had known in high school, then the onset of the rather painful awareness that Vivi had changed for the worse, followed by the full bloom of agony over the realization that she was rationalizing because she had never really known who Vivi was.

As a teenager, she had built an unsuspecting Vivi into her dream lover. She had needed one to get her through the long, lonely nights of adolescent lesbianism in Spruce Bay. But she should have realized that the Vivi of her dreams had been a construct, that it wasn't fair to her or to Vivi to presume that anything about this phantom lover had been true. She had moved away from home many years ago and hadn't bothered to look back long enough to divest herself of her illusions.

Dumb.

Double dumb.

Harry gazed into the mirror and ignored the wounded-doe look in her eyes as she combed her hair.

Just then, someone knocked on the door.

What, was this Grand Central Station, she wondered as she walked swiftly from the bathroom and opened it.

"I brought your car back," Mike said.

"Thanks," Harry said, surprised to see him. "I was going to ask someone to drop me at the yacht club after church. How'd you get the keys?"

"They were in the glove compartment," he replied, holding them out to her. "Eddie put them there."

"Well, you've saved me a trip," Harry added, taking the keys from him.

"Linda suggested it, actually," he told her. "The only thing is, you'll have to drop me at the United Church, because she's taken our car."

"No problem – I was just about to get a little exercise by walking there," Harry said. "I'm nearly ready. Want to come in for a minute?"

"Sure," he said, following her into her room.

"Excuse the mess," Harry said once they were inside, and she realized how untidy the room was. Her suitcase was lying open on the floor, the beds were unmade, her clothes were spread over the chair and dresser top, and the nearly empty bottle of rum was sitting on her bedside table. She wasn't sure whether it would be more conspicuous to casually shove it in a drawer or to let it stand where it was.

"I didn't think you were the type to drink by yourself," Mike commented, fingering the bottle.

"I'm not," Harry replied shortly. "I had company."

"Oh?"

"Yes," she confirmed, picking up her purse. She was damned if she was going to tell him another thing. Let him guess. "I'm ready."

"Good. I don't want to be late," he said. "It's my church, after all, and I'm taking part in the service."

Harry slid into the driver's seat, buckled her seatbelt, turned the key in the ignition and waited until Mike was buckled in before putting the car in gear. "I don't know if I'll ever get used to seeing you wearing a clerical collar," Harry commented as she drove out of the parking lot.

When he didn't say anything, Harry glanced at him to see if he was offended. He had a distant expression on his face, but he didn't look particularly irritated.

"Mike?"

"What?"

"Maybe this is way out of line, but what went on in your life? Why did you decide to become a minister?" Harry asked, turning on Main Street.

Mike looked questioningly at her.

"There's nothing like a little tour of Spruce Bay on a Sunday morning. Don't worry, we've got at least three quarters of an hour before the service starts," Harry said, lowering the window and noticing for the first time that it was a beautiful day. The sun was shining, although the air was characteristically humid.

"Seeing that bottle on your dresser makes me think that you're not particularly happy," Mike said.

"I asked first," Harry asserted.

"Don't get me wrong, I don't have anything against gay people," Mike went on. "I believe that people have the right to live as they want, and anyway, I'm quite aware that you don't have any choice in the matter."

"I suppose you became a minister because you were unhappy. What happened? Wasn't marriage to Linda and life in this charming village enough for you?" Harry asked viciously as she turned onto another street. There was one house which needed a coat of paint, and another and another – it was a shame, really.

"You don't have to feel guilty about it," Mike continued, staring out the front windshield. "Lots of people have a drinking problem. Maybe your career is going nowhere, or life is devoid of meaning, or you're having problems with your relationship," he added with a sideways glance.

Harry tried to control her temper; losing it would be the swiftest way to be defeated in this little game they were playing. She turned the corner, drove up Mill Road, made a left on Midget's Hill and headed out of town, waiting for him to protest. He didn't, which made her feel nervous, especially when she remembered Judy's entreaty to be careful. Someone had killed Wayne, and it could have been Mike. He'd had the opportunity, as he'd been outside most of the evening barbecuing steaks which never quite got completely cooked. He might have been driven to murder if he had found out about Linda's affair with Wayne.

Maybe she should drive back to town. It could be dangerous to be in the car alone with someone, especially now that they were driving through the woods. But, then again, she was driving. She was in control. If she felt like she was losing it, she could always stop the car and get out.

"Is that what's wrong?" Mike continued. "You've got problems with your love life."

"I'll thank you to leave my personal life out of this," Harry replied tersely, losing her temper despite her best intentions. "And I don't have a drinking problem. Vivi came over late last night and brought that bottle with her. If you want to talk with her about whether she has a drinking problem, then go right ahead, but if you mention it one more time, I'll stop the car and you can get out and walk back."

"I see," Mike said.

"No, I don't think you do," Harry replied. "I don't like being insulted."

"Well, neither do I, Harriet, neither do I," Mike replied.

"What?"

"I don't appreciate being treated like a creature from outer space," Mike explained, "and I'm sure you know what I'm talking about."

"I said I might be way out of line," Harry protested.

"That doesn't stop what you said from being insulting," he insisted.

"I thought people of the cloth knew how to turn the other cheek," Harry commented, knowing it was a low blow but saying it anyway.

"Smart-ass," he said, his voice surprisingly affectionate. "The truth is, my life was empty, and I turned to religion to fill it," he added calmly. "I know you probably can't understand that, but it's true."

Harry felt contrite but she didn't say anything. She had insulted him, he had insulted her, and if they continued like this, they would eventually have nothing more to say to each other, not even malicious diatribes. And it would be a pity, because she had always liked Mike. Even though he had run with the wild crowd, he hadn't looked down on those who hadn't. And last night at the cottage, Harry had felt nothing but good will toward him.

"Why don't you turn around so we can get to church on time?" he suggested. "Unless you were under the impression that the service was being held in Church Pond."

Harry gave him a look, then made a U-turn and drove back the way they had come. "Can we start over again?" she asked.

"Why not?" he agreed amiably.

"I'm just trying to understand what happened in your life," Harry said, picking her words with care.

"Why should it matter to you?" he asked. "We haven't seen each other in decades."

"I know," Harry replied. "But we grew up together, Mike, and I'm curious."

"Do you think I killed Wayne?"

Harry nearly drove off the road.

"Well, I didn't," Mike insisted.

"Oh."

"No matter what the reason, I could never harm another human being," Mike told her.

"What reasons are you talking about, Mike?" Harry asked.

"I prefer to be called Michael," he replied quietly.

The car creased Midget's Hill and she drove back into Spruce Bay.

"I don't like talking about my personal life," he said finally. "There was too much gossip in the old days, and now I'm careful about what I say. You of all people should know about stereotypes and how harmful they can be."

"You're right," Harry replied, glancing at him as she pulled into the church parking lot, parked the car and turned off the ignition. She was disappointed that he wasn't willing to tell her anything and upset by his gentle accusation that she had stereotyped him, because it was true.

"See you later," he said, getting out of the car.

Harry watched him walk into the United Church and then leaned over and rolled up the window on the passenger side. What a skilled investigator she was; at this rate, Judy would be right – she wouldn't get home until Christmas.

She got out and locked the car, looking at the church as she stuffed her car keys into her pants pocket. The building was white with black trim and had obviously been painted recently. Sea-going, god-fearing folk might neglect their homes, they might let the paint peel and their porches rot, they might not replace cracked window glass, but they'd respond generously to an appeal from the pulpit for extra donations to keep the church from falling down. Nobody considered that money filling the church coffers might put food in their children's mouths or pay the dentist or repair the unsafe brakes on the family car. That was simply how it was.

"Remember your manners," Harry muttered to herself, walking reluctantly toward the church. It seemed to loom over her, and she glanced up uneasily. Well, it *was* a tall building, with that spire and all. Churches traditionally were. And, as Judy would say, don't take things so personally. Organized religions and their houses of worship had not been put on earth simply to vex Harriet Hubbley, no matter how true she felt this to be. She stood outside the door and reminded herself that lots of queer people were religious, that they had come to an accommodation between one or another of the world religions and being queer. Just because she couldn't didn't mean that religion should be irrelevant to everyone or that Christianity was inimical to good mental health. It just felt that way to her.

She opened the heavy wood door and walked in. The contrast between the bright sunlight and the subdued lighting in the church blinded her temporarily, and she paused until her eyes acclimatized. Her nose began to twitch as she rapidly remembered another reason why she disliked churches. They were filled with flowers of every imaginable size, colour and scent. She reached into her purse for a tissue but sneezed before she could pull it out. Her sneeze echoed in the cavernous building, drowning out the carefully cadenced words of the minister, who was dressed in a white gown. That must be the Anglican, she thought absently as she wiped her nose.

Feeling like a trespasser with a runny nose, she walked up the middle aisle until she spotted her classmates about half-way from the altar and off to one side. They were sitting together, the men in suits and ties, some of the women in dresses and wearing hats. It didn't matter, Harry thought as she glanced down at her beige cotton pants suit. She didn't live here anymore, so let the gossip fly. With that mental dismissal of convention, she whispered excuse-me's to several parishioners seated on the aisle as she pushed past them and sat down next to Teresa Middleton.

"Hi," Harry whispered, feeling sweat break out on her forehead. The church was airless and humid, and the florid, funeral-like scent of flowers was overwhelming.

"Let's leave right now," Teresa whispered, grasping Harry by the arm.

"But I just got here," Harry protested to no avail. Teresa pulled on the sleeve of her jacket, forcing her to rise.

"Hurry," Teresa said gruffly.

Heads turned and people frowned at the disturbance. Teresa ignored them, so Harry did the same.

"Where are we going?" Harry asked, smiling apologetically at the people seated at the end of the pew as she followed Teresa past them. "Sorry, sorry," she whispered as she stepped on a foot and saw a woman wince.

Then she was walking down the aisle, following an obviously agitated Teresa, pausing to look back once as the choir began to sing. Vivi had turned and was staring at her, and Harry waved. Vivi nodded and turned to face the front of the church again.

"Come on," Teresa said, grasping her by the hand. Teresa's palm was hot and sweaty, and Harry wanted to let go of it, but Teresa was holding on too tightly. Teresa leaned against the heavy door to open it and pulled Harry through. Bright sunlight made Harry squint as she sneezed one last time.

"Air," she gasped thankfully.

"Hypocrites," Teresa said vehemently.

"I agree wholeheartedly," Harry said, moving away from the church.

"Mealy-mouthed cowards," Teresa continued, pacing back and forth in front of the door to the church. "Talking about Wayne as if he was a true son of God. They're afraid to mention hellfire and damnation. They would rather let their people sin and go straight to hell. Do you know what I'm talking about?"

Harry opened her mouth and closed it again.

"Only the Baptists are on the true road to salvation," Teresa continued without waiting for a reply. Harry was thankful, because she didn't have one. "You didn't know that did you?"

Please keep talking, Harry beseeched her mentally. Don't stop now, not until I can figure out a way to escape!

"But God doesn't differentiate. If the preachers don't point the true way to salvation, they're going to end up in hell, too," Teresa said emphatically. "For us to benefit from His everlasting mercy, God must be exceedingly strict. We must abide by His rules and by His commandments if we want to have any hope of going to Heaven."

Under cover of blowing her nose, Harry moved a little further away. It was the middle of the day, the sun was shining, but she felt as if she was lost in the fog of irrationality.

"But I digress," Teresa said, shaking herself like a terrier.

"What?" Harry said, resisting the urge to turn tail and run. She had wanted to question Teresa, and here was her opportunity. "I know you're not a religious person, Harriet," Teresa informed her. "But I've decided not to hold it against you."

"Thanks," Harry said, but her wryness was lost on Teresa, and not for the first time Harry wondered why so many religious people parked their sense of humour at the church door.

"Unlike most of our classmates, I think you have a strong sense of right and wrong," Teresa said as she stopped pacing and slowly approached Harry, who stepped back until she was leaning against her rental car.

"Really," Harry said breathlessly.

"I know who you are," Teresa said with a stern look on her face.

"Do you, now?" Harry asked, sweat running down her face. She slid away from the car and from Teresa and searched in her pocket for a tissue, pulling out her car keys instead.

"What a good idea," Teresa said as soon as she saw the keys. "Let's go for a drive."

"I don't think so," Harry said with a shaky laugh, pushing her keys back into her picket. "I was just looking for some tissue. I'm waiting for – for Linda."

"That bitch," Teresa said savagely.

"Take it easy," Harry begged. "She's my friend."

"Never mind," Teresa said, shaking herself again. "I'm fine. You should choose your friends more carefully. But I know what you are, and you can't help it."

"I'm going back to church," Harry said abruptly. She couldn't stand there and listen to this woman for one more second.

"Let's go for a drive," Teresa insisted.

"I told you that I have to wait for Linda," Harry said patiently.

"If you take me for a drive, I'll tell you who killed Wayne," Teresa said with a toothy smile.

Chapter 15

Harry stared at Teresa, who continued to radiate a weird goodwill. She didn't trust Teresa or her expression of unadulterated amity, and she didn't believe that Teresa knew who had killed Wayne. But her curiosity got the better of her.

"Tell me now, and then we'll drive to the police station together," Harry suggested. Even if there was any chance that Teresa had solved Wayne's murder, she wasn't reckless enough to get into the car with her. She would have to find out whether Teresa knew something in another way.

"I don't think so," Teresa replied. "But we could go for a walk."

"All right," Harry agreed instantly.

"We'll go down there," Teresa said, pointing toward the front harbour.

Harry followed her past the church and down the street. It was a short walk to the harbour, only three blocks. The tide was in, and the surface of the water was calm enough to reflect the clouds. Tiny waves lapped against the shore.

"Let's walk out on the wharf," Teresa suggested.

As Harry stepped on to the wharf, the smell of creosote bit into her nose. "I love that smell," she said to Teresa as she took a deep breath.

"Do you? I've always found it rather overpowering," Teresa replied.

How could Teresa be so normal one minute and so bizarre the next, Harry wondered. "Did you see something that night at the barbecue?" she asked once they had walked to the end of the wharf.

Teresa smiled enigmatically and sat down, her legs dangling over the edge.

Harry looked at the film of greasy dirt covering the wood planks of the wharf and reluctantly sat down. She hadn't been that fond of these pants anyway, she rationalized. She had tossed it into her suitcase at the last moment because she didn't have enough fancy clothes to wear. Now she could throw it out in good conscience.

"I wonder how deep it is right here," Teresa said, staring down into the water.

"I don't know," Harry replied, resisting the urge to move further away from the other woman.

"Did you ever go swimming in the front harbour?" Teresa asked.

"No," Harry replied, and then wondered why they never had. Perhaps it had been too polluted even then, she thought. People hadn't talked much about pollution in those days.

"Do you remember going swimming in the back harbour every summer?" Teresa asked.

"Sure," Harry replied at once. "How could I forget? We used to *live* down there."

"Yeah," Teresa said with a laugh.

Harry glanced at her, surprised to see the warmth in her eyes.

"I had two bathing suits," Harry reminisced, hoping Teresa would continue to relax. "I wore one in the morning for my swimming lessons and then when I went home for lunch, I changed into the other one, which I thought was better for lying around in the sand and suntanning."

"You were very popular," Teresa commented.

"I had some friends," Harry admitted, surprised that Teresa remembered. Teresa had been a loner. She had not been able to swim well and had never taken part in the raucous diving sessions off the end of the wharf to search for eels, which they fortunately rarely found, or the disorganized swimming matches they organized when enough of them were there, races invariably won by those who were willing to pull the other competitors under water and off stroke.

"Nobody swims in the back harbour now," Teresa told her.

"Why not?" Harry asked, leaning back and staring up at the sky. It was a beautiful shade of blue, and white fluffy clouds scudded high overhead.

"Untreated sewage has always poured into the back harbor not far from the swimming hole," Teresa replied.

Harry should have known. Even when they were in school there were rumblings about the sewage problem, and she could recall swimming in the back harbour at low tide and being reluctant to put her feet down in muck which all the kids jokingly said, and secretly believed, was human excrement.

"They built a swimming pool a few years ago," Teresa added, pointing toward the newer part of town.

"You mean there's nowhere to safely swim except the pool?" Harry asked incredulously.

"That's right," Teresa said, smiling at her.

"I don't believe it," Harry laughed. "That's like shooting yourself in the foot!"

"Exactly," Teresa said. "I thought you would see the irony in it."

It was pathetic, Harry thought, looking down at the water again. It looked so deceptively pure, like you could scoop some up with your hands and drink it. But the front harbour had suffered from years of industrial pollution; the fish plant, the foundry and the shipyards had always discharged their waste products into the water. And decades of raw sewage pouring into the back harbour had resulted in swimming being unsafe. What a tragedy. Spruce Bay was nearly surrounded by water and there was nowhere to swim but in an artificial swimming pool.

"So, who do you think killed Wayne Williams?" Teresa suddenly asked.

"You're asking me?" Harry answered. She hadn't been expecting that question. She had followed Teresa's lead in the conversation, hoping that she would calm down enough to talk lucidly about Wayne.

"Yes, you," Teresa said, turning to face Harry. "You're like the rest of them, aren't you?"

"I don't know what you mean."

"You think I'm crazy, don't you?" Teresa persisted.

Harry sighed.

"I won't tell you a thing unless you're truthful with me," Teresa said firmly. "I believe you owe me that."

She was talking about respect, Harry realized. Oh, lord, Mike had been right; she had typecast Teresa as a Protestant fundamentalist, which had all too easy to forget that she was a human being, not some one-dimensional religious puppet. "I'm sorry," she said contritely.

"That's not what I want," Teresa said.

"I don't think that you're crazy," Harry said, biting her upper lip. "I believe that you get carried away sometimes, and to somebody who's not into religion, it seems like you're about to lose control."

"You don't understand the power of God manifested through His disciples," Teresa replied.

"No," Harry said unequivocally.

"And you don't want to," Teresa added.

"No, I don't," Harry admitted. If this meant that Teresa wouldn't tell her what she suspected, then so be it. She wouldn't lie, not about something like that.

"I think that Bridget Andrews killed Wayne Williams," Teresa said, rising abruptly.

"What?" Harry exclaimed, scrambling to her feet and brushing off her backside.

"I was watching her Friday night," Teresa said as Harry caught up with her. "She was frantic."

"She tends to get like that sometimes," Harry said as they left the wharf, cut down the grassy slope, which led from the paved road to the old dirt path that followed the harbour, and walked along the shore.

"Don't forget that I grew up with you," Teresa reminded her, "So I've known Vivi Andrews for as long as you have. But she was different Friday night. She was drinking too much, which wasn't necessarily out of character, but the alcohol didn't relax her. She was quite agitated. And then I saw her walk out to the beach with Wayne. A little while later, she came back alone."

"That doesn't mean anything," Harry blustered, unwilling to believe that Vivi had killed Wayne, even though she herself had considered that possibility. Wayne and Vivi had likely wanted a little privacy, and what better place to find it than on the beach?

"Don't discount what I've said because you're a friend of Vivi's," Teresa warned her.

"I wouldn't do that," Harry protested.

"I have to go," Teresa said.

"But we're not finished talking!"

"I've had all I have to say," Teresa interrupted. "I have to go home now and prepare lunch for my family."

"Teresa," Harry said as her classmate walked away.

"What?" Teresa said, swinging around.

"Thanks."

Teresa nodded, turned the corner, and disappeared.

Damn. Harry felt like she was wading in mud that was thicker than the sludge in the back harbour. Could Vivi have murdered Wayne? She could believe that Vivi and Wayne had become lovers in high school and had secretly continued their relationship once they were in Toronto. But, no, she couldn't believe that Vivi had killed him.

There were too many suspects and not enough victims, she thought irreverently as she kicked a stone. "Shit," she muttered, lifting her foot. It hurt, and there was blood on it. She had forgotten that she was wearing sandals.

She climbed a tall rock on the edge of the water and sat on top of it. The skin on her face felt sunburned, her throat was dry, her foot hurt, and her heart ached. It was this last which troubled her the most. She didn't want Vivi to be a murderer. She also didn't want any of the others to be murderers – not Mike or Linda or Dan or Betty or Sandy or even Margaret, Eddie or Teresa. What she wanted more than anything else in the world was for Wayne to be alive. She would gladly put up with his vulgar taunts and his sly digs if he was only sitting there beside her.

"Harry."

She was so startled that she slid off the rock and went feet first into the water, breaking her fall with her hands.

"Shit!" she exclaimed, lifting her hands. Her palms were skinned and bleeding in a couple of places. She turned to give hell to whoever had startled her.

"Harry?"

"Judy!" Harry exclaimed, her wounds and drenched clothes forgotten.

"God, you're filthy! You look like you've been through a war!" her lover exclaimed.

Ignoring her myriad bruises and cuts, Harry single-mindedly waded to shore and wrapped her arms around Judy. "You don't know what this means to me," she murmured, close to tears.

"You're soaking wet. And bleeding," Judy said.

"I know," Harry replied, hugging her even tighter.

"I've been looking for you for ages," Judy said, kissing her on the cheek.

"What are you doing here?" Harry asked.

"I listened to what you said and took the next flight out, rented a car in Halifax, and drove right down here," Judy replied simply.

"Thank god," Harry muttered.

"Let's get you to the car," Judy said as they walked up the grassy slope to the road.

"Harriet! What happened? Did someone attack you?" Vivi asked anxiously as she rushed from the car.

"No. I fell into the water," Harry replied, glancing at Judy and trying not to grin when she saw the expression on her lover's face. Vivi hovered as Harry got into the front seat.

"What are you doing here?" Harry asked.

"Judy arrived at the motel just as I was returning from church, so I offered to help her find you," Vivi replied.

"Let's go back to the motel and dress those scratches on your hands," Judy said in the eminently sensible tone Harry recognized so well.

"But my car is back at the church," Harry answered. "If you drive me there, I can pick it up and meet you at the motel." And then something else occurred to her. "I haven't got my purse!" she exclaimed, trying to recall when she had last seen it. "I must have left it in the church when Teresa and I left."

"I saw you follow her down the aisle and I wondered what was going on," Vivi commented.

"She was indignant that the minister said such nice things about Wayne," Harry said, wondering how Vivi would react if she knew that Teresa had accused her of murder.

"How typical," Vivi said archly. "She's as crazy as a bedbug. Why, I wouldn't be a bit surprised if she was the one who killed Wayne."

"Actually, that's what she said about you," Harry remarked casually, waiting for an eruption of fireworks.

"How silly," Vivi replied with an artificial laugh. "But then she never liked me."

"I suppose," Harry said, surprised by Vivi's muted reaction.

"I think we'd better go to the church and look for your purse," Judy said as she opened the door on the driver's side and got into the car.

"I wonder if anyone found it," Harry worried. She wasn't as distressed about the tens and twenties in her wallet as she was about her driver's licence and her credit cards. Thank goodness she had thought to transfer her airline ticket to her suitcase.

"Oh, it's probably still there," Vivi said casually. "No one is going to steal a purse from a church. Not in Spruce Bay."

"Where can we drop you?" Harry asked Vivi.

"Have you already forgotten that I'm staying at the Barnacle Motel too?" Vivi reminded her. "How fickle, Harriet."

Harry ignored Judy's chuckle, closed her eyes, and wished she was somewhere else.

"However, it's such a nice day that I think I'll take a little walk along the harbour," Vivi said lightly.

"Suit yourself," Harry replied rather curtly, closing her door.

"I'll see you later," Viv said.

The car roared into life. Harry opened her eyes and watched Vivi walk down the grassy incline to the dirt path which followed the water. She suddenly wanted to giggle but stifled it by roughly rubbing her face with the back of her hand. She felt so relieved that Judy was there that if she started to laugh, she would probably never stop. Either that, or she would cry. It wouldn't be the first time.

Judy glanced at her, an amused look on her face, and then put the car in gear and drove off. "The two of you certainly have an interesting relationship," she commented.

"You sound surprised," Harry replied.

"She not exactly your type," Judy remarked, grasping one of Harry's hands in hers and turning it over. The bleeding had stopped, but Harry's palm looked raw.

"Vivi's just a little high strung. She's always been like that," Harry answered, ignoring how much her palms stung. Her foot hurt, too.

"Neurotic, you mean," Judy said, her voice void of inflection. Was she jealous? Harry glanced at her, but her expression wasn't giving anything away.

"Never mind," Harry said, unwilling to argue with Judy or to defend Vivi. She felt too uncomfortable physically to suspend that amount of energy. "Anyway, it's over with Vivi, and you're here now," she said, suddenly feeling shy. "I must look a holy mess," she said with a short laugh, running the fingers of her least damaged hand through her hair. It felt stiff with salt.

"You look fine," Judy assured her. "Tired, bruised, frightened, but fine."

"Frightened?"

"Yes, frightened," Judy replied. "But we'll talk about that later."

"I'm all right."

"Here we are. I keep forgetting what a small town this is," Judy said, driving into the church yard.

"Yes," Harry replied, swiftly looking away.

"Are you crying?"

"Of course not."

"Look at me."

"Don't be silly. Just wait a second and I'll run in and get my purse," Harry said, opening the door and stepping out before Judy could stop her.

She tried the front doors, but they were locked. She was undeterred, remembering from childhood that one of the side doors was always left unlocked to permit parishioners to enter. As kids, they used to sneak into the church and play hide-and-seek in the pews. She walked around to the side door, gratified to see that she had been right. It opened easily, and she slipped in. She stood just inside the door until her eyes adjusted to the dim light which filtered through the stained-glass windows. The church was silent as the grave, the air still and heavy, the sickly-sweet scent of flowers pervasive. Her nose twitched but she willed it to behave. She wasn't going to be there long enough for it to get itself into a dither.

As soon as she could see, she crossed the church. It was gloomy and the unnatural silence was spooky. There was a noise, a dull thud, which sounded as if it had come from behind her. She paused and looked around, but she could see no one. She decided that it must have come from outside.

She darted up the middle aisle, calculated approximately where she had been siting during the service, and went into that pew. She looked on the seat and the floor for her purse, but it wasn't there. Perhaps she had misjudged precisely where she had been sitting, she thought, bending over to look in the pew in front of her. Ah yes. There it was. She leaned over the back of the pew to pick it up when something heavy suddenly connected with her head. Her legs went out from under her, and she began to tumble forward. She tried to put her arms up to break her fall, but they wouldn't move. She was dropping like a stone and there wasn't a damn thing she could do about it. She felt as limp as a rag doll and then there was nothing.

Chapter 16

"Stay awake, Harry," Judy urged. "You're not allowed to sleep yet."

If Judy had a headache like this, she might want to be unconscious, too, Harry thought peevishly as she opened her eyes again.

"Good," Judy encouraged.

"Not really," Harry replied as she tried to focus.

"Who did this to you?" Judy asked.

Harry squinted carefully at her lover's face, saw concern but not terror, and relaxed. No matter how much her head hurt, Judy didn't think she was going to die. "I don't know," she whispered, her throat dry. "Where am I?" she asked, lifting her head a little and then letting it fall back on the pillow when the throbbing increased.

"In the emergency room of the hospital," Judy responded, squeezing her hand.

"My head hurts like hell. I feel like a tank ran over me," Harry said, gingerly flexing both arms and then her legs. They were stiff, but they all worked.

"Think a little, Harriet," came a deep male voice which Harry swiftly realized belonged to Chief Sandy Burns. "Can you tell us who tried to kill you?"

Harry's eyes opened wide. "Someone tried to kill me?" she asked, turning her head to look at him. She realized immediately what a dumb question that had been. People didn't get hit over the head for fun and pleasure.

"Seems like it," Constable Dalton said swiftly. Chief Burns turned and gave him a dirty look, which he ignored. "We found the weapon – it was a big, brass cross."

"Judy?" Harry said, her voice quivering. "Is it true? Somebody hit me over the head with a *cross*?"

"Yeah. It was a cross, believe it or not. We're checking it for prints now," Sandy confirmed. "Have you got any idea who would want to brain you with one of those things?"

"You've got a bump on the back of your head, but apparently it was only a glancing blow. You must have been in the process of bending over to pick up your purse when they hit you," Judy explained gently. "The doctor doesn't think you have

a concussion, although she wants to check you over again. She'll
be back in a couple of minutes."

"So. Do you know who did it?" Sandy asked, sounding
like a broken record.

"No," Harry replied.

"Oh, come on, Harriet, you must have noticed
something," Sandy said as he leaned over her. She wondered if
he meant to be in her face. "And what about you?" he asked,
turning to Judy. "Didn't you see anything?"

"No," Judy replied. "I was sitting in the car. Look, I
really think she needs to rest."

"And who are you?" Sandy asked, straightening up and
stuffing his thumbs in his belt.

"She's my partner," Harry replied swiftly. "My lover,"
she added, grateful that Judy moved closer to the gurney when
she heard the tension in Harry's voice, even though she couldn't
have entirely understood the cause. Harry wanted Sandy Burns
to know about her relationship with Judy in no uncertain terms,
especially after the acrimonious conversation they had had in the
deli.

Sandy looked furious. "I don't care who she is," he said
harshly. "I asked you a question, Harriet, and I expect an
answer."

"Is it customary for the police in this town to badger a
victim of a crime in this way?" Judy asked angrily.

"What are you talking about?" Sandy snapped with
unveiled hostility.

"I mean that Harry was attacked by someone who might
have been trying to kill her, and how you're browbeating her as
if it was her fault," Judy replied tersely.

"Well, I don't know about that," Sandy snarled. "And
you don't have any right to interfere in police business, Miss –"

"Judy Johnson," Judy told him. "Now just you listen
here, mister –"

"I happen to be the Chief of Police in this town," Sandy
blustered.

"And I happen to be an increasingly irate citizen," Judy
barked. "I'm sure this province has a Police Commission and
that they would be extremely interested in listening to a
complaint of police brutality."

"Police brutality?" Sandy roared, his face reddening.

"Police brutality?" Dalton squeaked. "Chief, perhaps we'd better give these girls a chance to regain their composure!"

"Po-lice bru-tal-ity?" Sandy repeated disbelievingly.

"Judy," Harry said urgently, tugging at Judy's sleeve. She remembered only too well that Sandy Burns had the disposition of a bulldog and that he was unbelievably tenacious once he got hold of something. Although that might be an insult to the intelligence of the ordinary garden-variety bulldog, she thought as she tried to sit up.

"I could have you arrested!" Sandy bellowed.

"Just you try it!" Judy retorted.

Harry succeeded in sitting up and produced the loudest moan she could muster, only some of it false.

"Harry! Are you all right?" Judy asked, her voice full of concern.

"What in earth is going on in here?" the doctor asked. "You! Lie back down!" she ordered Harry, who gladly obeyed. She fell back and closed her eyes, wishing that someone would switch off the overhead light. Her head felt like it was going to split, but her diversionary tactic had worked.

"And you, Sandy Burns – who gave you permission to come in here?" The doctor continued.

"Now, Nora, don't get riled," Sandy said, backing away from the hospital bed.

"Nora? Nora Hopkins?" Harry said, opening her eyes and looked more closely at the white-jacketed, middle-aged woman leaning over her. "You're a doctor?"

"Miracles never cease, do they, Harriet? Sorry I couldn't be at the reunion, but I've been on call all weekend," Nora responded.

"Confidentially, Nora, you haven't missed much," Harry replied.

"So I hear," Nora said with a detached smile as she concentrated on taking Harry's pulse. "It's a little fast," she said, dropping her wrist.

"No wonder," Judy grumbled.

"I heard shouting," Nora said, looking from Judy to Sandy.

"That woman is obstructing justice," Sandy contended, pointing at Judy.

"Don't be ridiculous," Norma scolded him. "Harriet has just been hit on the head and she's in no condition to be questioned."

"Precisely," Judy said.

Sandy glared at Judy but said nothing.

"Come back later," Nora said.

"How much later?" Constable Dalton asked.

"Why don't we call you?" Judy suggested.

"But – "

"That sounds perfect," Harry interjected. "I'll get in touch with you as soon as this wretched headache goes away."

Sandy looked outraged. He turned and stomped from the room, leaving a dazed-looking Constable Dalton spinning in his wake.

"If you'll excuse me, ladies," Constable Dalton said, but any attempt to make a dignified exit faltered when his voice cracked. He scurried after Chief Burns.

"Laurel and Hardy," Harry said.

"They lack Laurel and Hardy's wit and intelligence," Judy said with biting accuracy.

Harry heard Nora's faint chuckle. "How do you feel now, Harriet?"

"I wouldn't want to run the hundred-yard dash right this very moment," Harry replied.

"Your blood pressure is excellent," Nora said. "Now, just lie still while I shine this light in your eyes."

Harry did as she was told.

"Any dizziness? Nausea? Double or blurred vision?" Nora asked, finishing with one eye and moving on to another.

"No," Harry replied. "Just one hell of a headache."

"That's to be expected after a blow on the head," Nora explained.

"Does that mean I'm going to live?" Harry joked.

"For the next several decades, all things being equal," Nora replied. "Which means that you can afford to take it easy for a couple of days, right?"

"I don't think I have much choice," Harry replied.

"Probably not," Nora agreed. "Since you don't exhibit any symptoms of concussion, I won't make you wait for an x-ray."

"Can you give me something for the pain," Harry asked.

'Unfortunately, no," Nora said. "If there is anything wrong, we certainly don't want to mask it."

Great, Harry thought. She was going to have to solve Wayne's murder while suffering from a giant-sized headache. She sat up, stifling a groan.

"I meant it when I said that you must take it easy," Nora warned. "And if you do start to feel nauseated, dizzy or you begin to experience double vision, get back here as soon as possible. A concussion is nothing to ignore – it can have serious consequences."

"Okay," Harry conceded.

"I've disinfected and dressed the scratches on your hands and the cut on your foot. Those should heal swiftly – your hands will probably be sore for a day or two, a bit stiff and even itchy as they heal, but you shouldn't have any problem with them. But a headache caused by a bump on the head can last from a few days to a week, and if you don't take care of yourself by resting, it could linger for much longer."

"I hear you," Harry remarked, her shoulder slumping. "It is safe to fly?"

"I think so. But give me a call before you schedule your flight," Nora suggested.

"It's already scheduled," Harry replied. "I'm supposed to fly to Montreal tomorrow, but then again, Chief Burns has told us that we can't leave town until the police discover who killed Wayne Williams."

"Then you're not leaving tomorrow," Nora said.

None of them laughed, which was disheartening.

"Tell me, Nora, how did you go from being Canada's up-and-coming opera star to Nora Hopkins, MD?" Harry asked.

"Contrary to expectations, it's not a very long story," Nora said, smiling at Harry. "I realized shortly after I started my studies at the Conservatory of Music in Toronto that I wasn't quite good enough to make it to the top. I abhorred the idea of teaching music, so I dropped out, spent a couple of months sulking, and then registered in science at the University of Toronto, where I went on to do my medical degree."

"Wow!" Harry said.

"Wow?" Nora echoed, sounding puzzled.

"She's impressed, doctor, that's all," Judy said. "And she's too woozy to hide it."

"Let me tell you a secret," Nora said to Judy. "Harriet never could conceal much of anything."

"That's not true," Harry claimed. "It's not true at all, Nora Hopkins, and you know it."

Was she doomed to live through days if not weeks of feeling like she was distanced from everything going on around her because of the pain? Maybe she could write a book about the zen of headaches.

Judy and Nora shared a laugh that was too companionable for Harry's liking. She had never pegged Nora for a lesbian, but she could easily have been wrong. "When did you come back to Spruce Bay?" she asked Nora.

"Not all that long ago, actually," Nora said. "I've been here for about five years. I know it's become almost trite to put down Toronto, but I did grow tired of it. Perhaps it was the small fish in a big pond syndrome, which negatively affects so many Maritimers. When my sister told me that they were looking for someone to replace Dr. Simons when he retired, I jumped at the opportunity."

"Nora, did you ever run across Vivi Andrews or Wayne Williams when you were in Toronto?" Harry asked.

"Of course," Nora said, sounding startled. "Didn't Vivi tell you?"

"Tell me what?" Harry asked, battling her headache, which seemed to get worse whenever anyone asked her a question which required thinking.

"Why, we never really lost touch with one another. We had an informal sort of South Shore dinner club, as we laughingly used to call it," Nora replied. "We made a point of getting together every month or two. Of course, I was often on duty and couldn't get away, so sometimes I'd go several months without seeing either of them."

"Vivi never mentioned it," Harry said.

"Oh, well," Nora commented casually, although Harry thought she was surprised. "I suppose it must have slipped her mind."

Who was she trying to fool, Harry wondered. Vivi couldn't possibly have forgotten something like that, especially once Wayne had been murdered. And why was Nora protecting Vivi? "Judy, would you mind bringing the car around so I don't have so far to walk?" Harry asked.

Judy looked like she was about to remind Harry that the car was parked right in front of the hospital, but then she caught on. "Sure," she responded, "no problem."

"Thanks," Harry said with a smile.

"I'll be back in a couple of minutes," Judy said, leaving the room and closing the door behind her.

"Ok, Nora, time to ante up," Harry said, gingerly sliding her legs over the side of the bed.

"I don't know what you mean," Nora replied as she washed her hands.

"Of course you do," Harry said, trying to sound friendly. "Look, there don't have to be any secrets between us. After all, you've already probed and prodded my body, so you know what there is to know without carving a piece out of it."

"What are you talking about?" Nora asked.

Harry took a deep breath and regretted it because it made her headache flare. She had never suffered from a headache like this before; if she had been asked to put a colour to it, she would have said it was red. Bright red. "You disappoint me."

"Look, I don't know why she didn't tell you," Nora admitted, turning to face Harry.

Harry was about to nod but thought the better of it. She didn't know what came after red, and she didn't want to find out. "Why are you protecting Vivi?"

"Is it really any of your business?"

"No," Harry acknowledged.

"Then why are you asking?"

"I want to see if I'm right," Harry replied truthfully.

"About what?"

Harry didn't want to say. If she was wrong, Nora was bound to be angry. But is she kept things to herself, she would never find out who had killed Wayne.

"Well?"

Harry took a deep breath. "You were having an affair with Vivi, weren't you?"

"Don't tell me you figured that out by yourself," Nora laughed cynically. "She must have told you."

"She told me nothing," Harry said, trying to keep the harshness from her voice.

"I don't believe you," Nora said.

"Let me put it this way, then. Vivi told me what she wanted me to know," Harry amended.

"Which was what?"

That Harry was the first woman lover Vivi had ever had. And Harry, dumb bunny that she was, had believed her. "That she'd never had a woman lover," Harry finally answered.

"Before you, you mean," Nora said.

Harry looked up at her.

"Yes, that is what you mean," Nora confirmed, a weary look on her face, like she too had heard it all before.

How ignoble, Harry thought dourly. Pretty soon everyone in town would know that Vivi had put one over on her. But Vivi had been on top ever since they had played together in the sandbox in her back yard when they were just out of diapers. What else was new?

"So, she lied," Nora said with a sympathetic smile. "Don't look so depressed. We all know that Vivi has always molded the truth to her own advantage."

Yes, of course. But what she hadn't realized was that her dream lover bore more resemblance to the lover from hell than anyone else. "And Wayne? I suppose you had an affair with him, too," Harry said, completely exasperated.

"No," Nora replied emphatically. "Not that he didn't ask. Wayne would have slept with any woman who would have had him. But I turned him down."

No headache could have distracted Harry from the fact that Nora was telling the truth. "Sorry."

"That's all right," Nora said with a sigh.

There was a knock on the door and Judy came in. "Ready?"

"Yes," Harry replied, gingerly stepping down from the hospital bed.

"Let me help you," Judy said, grasping her by the arm.

Harry let go of the bed and put her weight on Judy.

"Now remember, take it easy," Nora reminded her. "And if you start to feel dizzy or nauseated or if you see double, come back to the emergency department. And try to stay awake until the time you usually go to bed."

"Yes, doctor," Harr replied meekly.

"Don't you 'doctor' me," Nora said with a laugh.

"Thanks, Nora," Harry said. "It's good to see you again. I hope you can make it to Linda and Mike's."

"I'm certainly going to try," Nora said, holding out her hand.

Harry shook it, and, holding Judy's arm, made her way from the hospital.

"Do you feel up to talking to the police now, or do you want to wait until later?" Judy said once Harry was safely seated in the passenger seat of her rental car.

"You're kidding, right? I feel like a truck is driving through my head," Harry said, holding a hand in front of her eyes. "Where's my purse? I need my sunglasses."

"I put it in the trunk," Judy said through the open window. "Hold on a second."

Harry cursed under her breath. She hated pain. Even mild menstrual cramps made her want to take to her bed. Judy said she likely had a low pain threshold, but still.

"Here," Judy said, getting into the driver's seat and handing Harry her purse. "Harry, I realize from personal experience that the police in this town leave everything to be desired, but you were attacked."

"Later," Harry said, putting on her sunglasses. They helped, but not much. "I need to get out of the sun. Maybe I'll feel better after sitting still for a couple of hours."

Judy looked at her, nodded, and drove back to the motel. As Judy helped her out of the car and into their room, Harry thought she saw the curtain open and then close in one of the other units and wondered whether it was Vivi's. She decided to ignore it; with her head throbbing the way it was, Vivi was the last person she wanted to see.

"I'm so glad you're here," she whispered as Judy piled several pillows against the wall. She sat on the bed and gingerly leaned back against them.

"So am I," Judy replied. "Will it bother you if I sit here beside you or would you prefer me to use the other bed?"

"Don't be silly – I want you close to me," Harry told her.

Judy sat down beside her. "I don't know what I would have done if you'd been seriously hurt," she whispered, burying her face in Harry's neck.

"Well, I wasn't, so don't even think about it," Harry said.

"You could have been killed," Judy said, her voice muffled.

"Shhh," Harry slowly turned her head so she could kiss Judy on the cheek. "Let's talk about something else."

But they didn't talk. It would have been superfluous. Harry held her lover in her arms and felt Judy's body gradually relax until she knew Judy had fallen asleep. Her headache gradually receded so she could almost pretend that it belonged to someone else, but she stopped herself from dozing.

Her thoughts were intensely circular. *Someone had tried to kill her*. It was so impossibly wrong that it wouldn't sink in. She couldn't connect it to her own mortality, so she played with the concept by creating scenarios. Perhaps she had lost her balance and tumbled head-first into the pew in front of her. Or something had fallen from the ceiling of the church and hit her skull. Or a giant seagull flying around the rafters of the church had taken a dump on her head, which now had five or six staples in it. Just the thought of those pieces of metal sticking into her skull made her skin crawl.

Who could have known that she was at the church, Harry wondered suddenly.

Vivi. She had said she wanted to go for a walk, but when had Vivi ever freely chosen to engage in any type of physical activity? And she had been there when Harry had realized that her purse was missing. Vivi could have followed them on foot to the church and attacked her. But why? Vivi wouldn't hurt one of her lovers, would she?

Harry sighed and cautiously shifted her weight. Judy murmured in her sleep and tightened her arms around Harry. Most murders were committed by people the victims knew, although most of the perpetrators were men, not women. But she had to stop being so ambivalent about Vivi. Still, it was a fine kettle of fish to suspect a woman she had made love with less than forty-eight hours ago of having tried to bash her head in.

Who else might have known where she was?

Mike was the minister of the United Church. He could have been in his office when she went in search of her purse, doing whatever it was that ministers do after the church service was over. Changing clothes, opening the offering envelopes and counting the money people had stuffed into them, returning phone calls. He would know the church as well as his own home – the shortest way to each spot, where troublesome air currents flowed, where floorboards squeaked. He could have heard her enter the church, crept up behind her without her noticing and swatted her on the head.

She could imagine Mike in his black robe, with his clerical collar encircling his Adam's apple, stalking her like a humanoid crow, a brass cross clenched in his fist. And as he drew nearer, his muscular arm rising higher and higher until it swooped down, the cross crushing flesh – her flesh … She shivered and banished the image from her mind.

Linda could have done it, too. A minister's wife would be capable of navigating the church nearly as well as the minister himself, perhaps even better if she arranged flowers, sang in the choir or was a member of one of the women's circles. Although, upon reflection, Harry rather doubted that Linda was involved in such churchy things.

Okay, she thought, yawning. Vivi, Mike and Linda. Who else? Well, Dan and Betty lived across the street from the United Church, so it could have been either of them. When it came right down to it, any one of her classmates who had attended the ecumenical church service could have bashed her on the head, she thought suddenly. She had left her purse in the church and her rental car in the parking lot, and, logically, she would most likely come back to search for her purse and pick up her rental car at the same time. As for the side door through which she had entered, they all knew about that. Every single one of them, whether they were United Church parishioners or not, had tiptoed through that door at one time or another as a child, hands over their mouths to keep from giggling out loud as they plotted another bit of innocent childish deviltry. As with Wayne's murder, they had all possessed the opportunity. The question was, why would someone want her dead? Had she discovered something significant without realizing it?

"Don't fall asleep," Judy urged.

"Huh?" Harry muttered, once again growing aware of the throbbing inside her head.

Nora told you to stay awake," Judy said, giving her a gentle hug.

"My head hurts," Harry moaned.

"I know," Judy responded sympathetically. "What can I do?"

"Nothing," Harry sighed. "I'd just like to catch the person who did this to me."

"Who do you think it was?" Judy asked, running her hands up and down Harry's back.

"I have no idea," Harry replied. "Not yet, anyway. But that sure feels good."

"I'm glad," Judy purred. "Does your head feel any better?"

"No, Harry admitted, slipping her hand inside Judy's bra. "But I could be distracted."

"Wonderful," Judy murmured as they kissed, "although I don't think that this is what the doctor ordered. At least not now."

Harry sighed because Judy was right; however much she wanted to, she was incapable of making love. Even the thought that Judy had likely made love with Sarah this weekend couldn't rouse her to action. It was when she realized that she was incapable of reclaiming her lover that she really got angry. Someone was going to pay for this, she thought furiously. It had been a long time since she had been unable to make love – years, actually. And that had been pre-Judy, with a woman she had picked up at a gay bar after she'd had too much to drink. It wasn't fair, she thought as she removed her hand from Judy's bra. She wanted to make love, she really did. Her spirit was willing, but her flesh was weak through no fault of her own.

"There's a party later this afternoon," she said to Judy as she carefully disengaged herself from her lover, "and I want to go."

"I don't think you should," Judy replied. "You heard what the doctor said."

"I don't plan to race them around the block, although I wouldn't mind taxing their clogged arteries," Harry retorted, moving carefully to stop her head from exploding. "But since I'm not capable of doing that, I'm going to try to out-think them. What I need you to do is to find out when the party at Mike and Linda's is going to start."

Chapter 17

Harry and Judy spent the rest of the afternoon talking. Or, rather, Harry talked and Judy listened and synthesized what Harry told her about her classmates and asked pertinent questions with the intent of helping Harry clarify her thoughts.

"I think it would be easier to sort things out if we tackled them one at a time," Judy suggested. "Otherwise, we're just going to keep going round in circles."

"How right you are," Harry replied with feeling. "Could you refill my glass?"

"Sure," Judy said, getting up from the easy chair which she had pulled close to the bed.

"And this facecloth isn't cold anymore," Harry said, removing it from her forehead. Perhaps it was just wishful thinking, but it did seem to have some effect. Her headache was still there, but her head was no longer throbbing.

"If your headache is better, perhaps you should give it a rest," Judy said, walking into the bathroom to fill Harry's water glass.

"Maybe," Harry replied. "I don't know. I should have asked Nora."

"Let's get on with it, then," Judy said, placing the full glass of water on the bedside table. "As you quite correctly put it, everyone who was there Friday night had the opportunity to kill Wayne. People seem to have imbibed an inordinate amount of alcohol, everyone was in and out of the house with great frequency, and hours passed without their being anything so organized as a sit-down dinner or even a gathering around a campfire or a communal swim on the beach."

"We were getting reacquainted, so there was a lot of wandering from group to group," Harry agreed.

"If we can't place the murderer at the scene of the crime, then let's look at their motives," Judy suggested.

"I've tried to find out why each of them might want to kill Wayne, but the more I learn, the more confused I get," Harry said. "Most of them also seem to have a strong aversion to telling the truth."

"I suppose you're learning the first axiom of detecting," Judy said, sounding somewhat amusing.

"Which is what?" Harry asked, taking a sip of water from her glass.

"People lie," Judy replied.

Harry laughed and then thought better of it when her headache flared.

"Are you all right?" Judy asked, reaching out to touch her.

"Yes," Harry sighed. "But it's a damn shame when it hurts too much to laugh."

"It will pass," Judy reassured her. "You have to be patient."

"Ah, yes. My middle name," Harry joked.

"Never mind. Now, let's get down to business," Judy said. "Why don't we start with Mike and Linda. Tell me why either of them would want to kill Wayne."

"Linda was having an affair with him," Harry said. "One of which started in high school and was revived whenever Wayne returned to Spruce Bay."

"Perhaps she was madly in love with him and killed him when he told her he wanted to break up with her," Judy commented.

"Linda?" Harry said with a smile. "I don't think she's capable of being madly in love with anyone but herself."

"You should know, I suppose," Judy said. "But what if Wayne had threatened to tell Mike about their relationship?"

"That doesn't sound like much of a reason to kill someone," Harry replied.

"Don't be silly," Judy responded. "You read the newspapers and watch the news on television the same as I do. People are murdered every day for precisely for that reason."

"I suppose so," Harry said sceptically.

"Take my word for it. They are. Now, let's continue," Judy said.

"You like doing this, don't you?" Harry said suddenly.

"I suppose I do," Judy replied slowly. "It appeals to my need to organize things."

"Like doing crossword puzzles," Harry said.

"You're quite right," Judy answered with a smile.

"You should be the detective, then," Harry asserted. "I haven't got a head for this at all."

'Don't be silly," Judy scoffed. "I might be good at synthesizing, but I would never be able to think of what questions to ask. That's quite a talent, I hope you realize. I know I wouldn't have the nerve to ask people about their personal affairs. But that's neither here nor there. Whether it's good luck or bad, by design or by default, you're the detective in this family. Let's get back to Linda and Mike. Linda isn't the only one with a motive to kill Wayne. Mike could have done it out of jealousy."

"Yes, but it's not clear to me whether Mike knew that Linda was having an affair with Wayne. She told me that she kept things as quiet as possible, and although Mike might have suspected that she was sleeping around, he had no idea about Wayne."

"Do you believe her?"

"I believe she thinks it's true," Harry replied slowly.

"What if Mike discovered Linda and Wayne in bed together the day of the barbecue?" Judy asked.

"But he didn't get home until late," Harry objected. "There was a sudden death in one of the families in his congregation."

"Ah, but perhaps that's what he wanted you to believe," Judy remarked. "And maybe that's what he wanted Linda to think, too. But he could have arrived home unexpectedly without them noticing that he was there. They were busy making love, after all. Most people tend to concentrate when they're doing that."

"Do tell," Harry said dryly.

"Be serious," Judy chucked. "Anyway, Mike could have looked in the bedroom and left as soon as he realized what was going on."

"I suppose it's possible," Harry agreed. "When I drove him to church this morning, he wasn't willing to talk about his personal life at all. He told me that he didn't kill Wayne, though."

"What did you expect him to do, confess?"

"Of course not," Harry replied. "Still, minister or not, he's still just an ordinary guy from a village who's been steeped in centuries of puritanical bull. The sight of the two of them in bed together could have infuriated him, especially since he and Linda were expecting guests to arrive soon. What if someone had arrived early and discovered them in bed? Linda's thoughtlessness must have enraged Mike."

"You seem to be building a case for Mike having killed Linda, not Wayne," Judy commented.

"You're right," Harry said with a frown.

"Although if Mike was still in love with Linda, he might not have been capable of doing that," Judy added.

"It's not a very strong case, though," Harry concluded glumly. "There are too many ifs, buts and maybes. Mike might not have known. And if he did, he might not have cared. It just isn't clean."

"I agree, but that's as far as we can go with them on the information we have," Judy said. "Who's next?"

"Let's do Betty and Dan," Harry said in a rather casual fashion, as if they were comparing the price of tea in two different specialty shops.

"Betty would seem to have much the same motive as Linda," Judy commented. "And Dan's motives would be similar to Mike's."

"If you believe what Margaret said about Betty and Wayne carrying on a clandestine affair when we were in high school," Harry agreed. "But I'm not sure that I do."

"What, do you think that Wayne was sneaking into Betty's for something other than sex?" Judy asked.

"Could be," Harry replied.

"Like a frenzied game of monopoly?"

"More like Betty helping Wayne with his homework and he didn't want anyone to know about it," Harry replied with a grin. "Wayne was smart, but he bragged that he never studied. He didn't want people to think that he cared, even when he got good marks without ever appearing to open his books."

"I suppose that makes sense," Judy conceded.

"Not everything has to revolve around sex," Harry pointed out.

"Why Harry, I don't believe you said that," Judy teased. "Can I quote you?"

"Never mind," Harry growled. "But even if Margaret was right and Betty and Wayne were having sex in her living room when her parents were out, that was a long time ago. Why would either one of them want to kill Wayne at this late a date?"

"They would have been meeting all along, like Linda and Wayne," Judy suggested.

"But no one has mentioned it," Harry objected.

"Not yet."

"True."

"What if Wayne was nosing around and told Dan about their affair?" Judy proposed.

"Maybe," Harry said. "Still, why would Wayne say anything? And even if he did, would Dan care? He would probably tell Wayne to go shove it. After all, a lot of water has passed under the bridge since then. And we've all done things in our youth that we regret."

"Speak for yourself," Judy retorted.

"Yes, O Perfect One," Harry kidded, finishing her water. Her headache was subsiding, although it could simply be that she was distracted by their conversation. But maybe Nora had been wrong; maybe she wouldn't suffer for days. She gingerly turned her head and when it didn't start to throb, she turned it in the other direction. Then she stood up.

"Are you all right?" Judy asked.

"For the moment," Harry replied, sitting down again. So far, so good.

"Don't overdo it," Judy warned. "You need to conserve your strength for this evening."

"I know," Harry answered. "Look, we're not getting anywhere with Betty and Dan for the same reason we can't make any headway with Linda and Mike. We don't know who knew what, and when they knew it."

"You're right," Judy said with a sigh. "Who's next?"

"Well, there is Sandy Burns," Harry suggested.

"Lord, would I ever like him to be the one," Judy said with feeling. "What's his motive, though?"

"Wayne had an affair with Sandy's wife when they were in high school," Harry answered.

"Is there anyone Wayne didn't sleep with?" Judy asked incredulously.

"Margaret and Teresa seem to have resisted," Harry replied. "And me, of course."

"I suppose there's no evidence that Sandy Burn's wife …"

"Julia," Harry interjected.

"That Julia's affair with Wayne continued after high school."

"No," Harry said glumly. "An added complication is that Julia walked out on Sandy last winter."

"Then it's not likely that Sandy did it."

"I would think not," Harry agreed. "Unless there's something we don't know about."

"There's always that," Judy conceded. "Of course, that could be true of any or all of them."

"That's encouraging," Harry grumbled.

"But true," Judy said. "So, who's left?"

"Margaret, Eddie and Teresa were at the barbecue," Harry said, "but I don't really suspect any of them. And then there's Vivi," she began reluctantly.

"Whom you don't particularly want to discuss," Judy said.

Harry glanced at her, but she couldn't decipher the look on her lover's face. "She could have killed him."

"I know," Judy said, staring at Harry.

"What did you think of her?" Harry couldn't help asking.

"I didn't much like her," Judy replied, looking ill at ease. "I thought she was superficial and silly. But I was only with her for a short period of time, and she was obviously uncomfortable with me. But it doesn't matter what I think about her."

"No," Harry said slowly.

"She's staying here now, too. Why do you think she left Betty and Dan's?" Judy inquired. "After you moved out, she would have had your room all to herself."

"I don't know," Harry admitted. "But they've got eight kids. Maybe she got tired of waiting in line to use the bathroom."

"Perhaps it was her way of trying to get together with you," Judy suggested.

"Are you kidding?" Harry said with a laugh, flinching when her headache erupted momentarily. "Vivi wouldn't bother to use artifice – she'd just put all her cards on the table, and then take her clothes off and throw herself at me. Hey – just kidding!" she reassured her lover when she saw that Judy looked disconcerted. "Actually, she'd throw herself at me and leave it up to me to take her clothes off."

"If you weren't injured, I'd throw something at you and it wouldn't be me or my clothes," Judy declared.

"I love you, too," Harry said tenderly.

"Just checking, were you?" Judy asked.

"I don't know what you mean," Harry replied innocently.

"I'm sure," Judy said calmly, making a face at her.

"I wish we could make love," Harry said suddenly, feeling unreasonably deprived.

"Soon," Judy promised.

They stared at each other until Harry thought she would burst. "Where were we?" she asked, her voice husky. It was good that, after eleven years, her desire for Judy was fresh and strong. Now all she had to do was to remember that fact when they were back in the fray of their over-extended lives, with Judy's other lover in the picture.

"We were talking about Vivi," Judy reminded her.

"She has to be pretty high on our list of suspects," Harry said. "She's been in touch with Wayne all along. They were lovers, which wasn't a problem until Vivi married her second husband."

"And from the way you described it, she isn't in love with her husband," Judy added.

"True," Harry agreed. "The fact that he was well-to-do was more important than anything else. But Wayne was probably clinging to her like a leech, especially once she had access to money. He wouldn't be likely to disappear on command, either. He probably laughed when she told him to get lost. Wayne would do that."

"He sounds like a charming character," Judy commented.

"The funny thing was that sometimes he was. And at other times, you wanted to kill him," Harry told her. "So to speak," she hastened to say with an abortive laugh when she remembered that someone actually had. Sometimes it was hard to believe that Wayne was dead. Murder was something that happened to other people or in books or on television, not to someone she had grown up with. She raised her hand to her forehead and rubbed it, but it didn't do any good. "I guess you had to be there."

"Every class has someone like that in it," Judy commented.

"Every group, actually," Harry replied. "But Wayne was in a league of his own."

"Let's keep going," Judy suggested.

"Well, Vivi could have decided to kill him to keep him from making trouble with her new husband. He also could have wanted to borrow increasingly large amounts of money now that she was married to someone who had it," Harry postulated.

"That's an interesting idea."

"When I drove Wayne from Halifax to Spruce Bay, he was quite vague about what he did for a living," Harry continued. "Perhaps he was living off other people."

They stared at each other, awareness growing.

"Maybe Wayne was blackmailing Vivi," Harry said excitedly.

"Why just Vivi? Why not all of them?" Judy suggested.

"Honey, you're a genius," Harry exclaimed.

"Just slow down. We don't know for sure that Wayne was blackmailing anyone," Judy warned her. "And if you jump to conclusions, you might miss something important."

"You're right,' Harry conceded.

"You have to be careful," Judy admonished. "You've been poking around in people's personal affairs and asking questions which obviously offended someone who has already killed once."

Harry knew that. But she couldn't let the fear of danger paralyze her and prevent her from continuing. If she didn't remain determined, single-minded and fearless, she would never find out who had killed Wayne.

"You will be careful," Judy repeated like a mantra.

"Of course," Harry reassured her, hoping she sounded convincing.

Chapter 18

The telephone rang.

Harry reached for it and recoiled as pain rocked her head.

"Hello," Judy said, and then handed the phone to Harry. "It's for you. It's Betty."

Harry took a deep breath and took the phone from her lover.

"Are you all right?" Betty asked. "I heard that someone attacked you!"

"Yes, in the church this morning after the service. I went back to get my purse," Harry replied.

"That's what Sandy told Dan," Betty said, "but I couldn't believe it."

"I'm fine," Harry assured her. "Nora Hopkins checked me out at the hospital. I've got one hell of a headache, though. Listen, I'd like to come over for a little while."

There was a slight hesitation and then Betty said, "Sure. Maybe we can go to Linda and Mike's together."

"I'll see you soon, then," Harry said, handing the receiver back to Judy.

"Why do you want to go there first?" Judy asked as she replaced the receiver.

"So you can meet them and see the house," Harry replied. "And I'd like to have some time with Betty and Dan before the whole group gets together again."

"All right," Judy said, glancing at her watch and then getting up. "I guess I'd better change. You should too, if we're going to go directly from Betty and Dan's to the party. And how are you going to manage? I saw how you flinched every time you moved."

"I'll be okay if I remember not to move too quickly," Harry assured her. She eased her legs off the side of the bed and slowly got to her feet.

"How do you feel?" Judy asked.

"Okay. And don't worry, I'm not dizzy at all," Harry said. "If I was, I'd be on my way back to the hospital. I can't say that I feel like a million dollars, but my head doesn't hurt any more now than it did when I was sitting down."

"You know what, Harry?" Judy said, following Harry into the bathroom.

"What?" Harry asked as she stared at herself in the mirror. She gingerly turned her head, trying to see where she had been whacked. "It's still got blood all over it!" she exclaimed.

"I know," Judy answered calmly.

"Wash it off!" Harry shouted.

"Tomorrow," Judy responded. "I don't think we should touch it tonight."

"But I can't go out looking like this!" Harry exclaimed.

"Sure you can," Judy replied. "It will be a not-so-subtle reminder that you were attacked. It might be to our advantage if everyone is a little nervous, especially the killer."

"Maybe," Harry said dubiously.

"On the other hand, it might be so dark that no one will notice," Judy said.

"Fat chance," Harry grumbled, washing her face. "Sunset isn't for hours yet."

"Harry, do you remember Agatha Christie's *Murder on the Orient Express*?" Judy asked.

"Of course I do," Harry replied.

"Well, pretty darn near everyone who was at the barbecue Friday night had a reason to kill Wayne. What if it was a group effort?"

"You're kidding, right?" Harry said as they left the washroom. She watched Judy open the closet door and take out a brown blouse and her favorite beige pantsuit. "Do you think they formed a collective and drew lots to see who was going to bash him on the head? Or did they line up in alphabetical order like we did in school and swat him one after the other?"

"You figure it out – you're the detective," Judy said with a chuckle.

"Right! Pass the buck – see if I care," Harry laughed, trying to hide a shudder as pain shot through her head. "Now let's get serious. Help me decide what to wear."

Harry's wardrobe had suffered from serious attrition. The suit she has worn to church was filthy, and she would have thrown it in the garbage except for Judy's protest that her cleaner back in Montreal would be able to return it to its pristine condition. She inspected the clothes hanging in her closet, growing more irritated by the second. Someone had wanted to hurt her, to teach her a lesson, to make her stop asking questions, so what difference did it make what she wore? She was past the point of pretending to be someone she wasn't. It didn't work, anyway. Everyone always figured out that she was a lesbian. Maybe it was her short hair or the way she walked or the glint in her eye. She didn't know, and she didn't particularly care. She put on a pair of black jeans and a black vest over a white tee-shirt which she had bought last summer at the Stratford Festival. It had a picture of Gertrude Stein on the front.

"Are you sure that's what you want to wear?" Judy asked.

"Do you mind?"

"Of course not."

"It would be better if I still smoked. Then I could stomp around with a cigarette hanging out the corner of my mouth. But this will have to do," Harry remarked.

"I don't think you're going to be doing much stomping," Judy said.

"You're right," Harry replied, remembering the hole in her head.

"Besides, I'll divorce you if you ever start smoking again," Judy warned.

"I know, I know," Harry responded. She went into the bathroom and combed what hair she could, but that didn't help much. She considered asking Judy for some makeup, blusher especially, as her face was paler than usual, but she finally decided to stop being vain and to go as she was.

They arrived at Betty and Dan's a couple of minutes later. Judy parked and Harry got out of the car, glancing momentarily at the United Church. She had forgotten to call Sandy Burns, she thought suddenly as she rang the doorbell. He was not going to be pleased.

"Come in," Betty said, opening the door and then backing up. "Don't stand there all night, it's damp. You look horrible, Harriet. I'm surprised Nora didn't put a patch on that wound. Actually, I suppose she couldn't – it would pull your hair out. Are you sure you should be up walking around?"

"I'm fine," Harry replied. "And don't worry. Nora said to take it easy, which is what I'm doing."

"Who is this you've brought with you?"

"This is my partner, Judy Johnson," Harry said, putting her arm around Judy.

"Nice to meet you. Harry's told me so much about you and your family," Judy said.

Betty's eyes widened and then her instincts as a good hostess took over. "Nice to meet you, too," she said, taking Judy's hand and giving it a firm shake. "Dan? Harriet's here. Now you just go right on into the living room and Dan will make you drinks. I have to check on the kids for a minute and then I'll be down to join you."

"Dan! Good to see you," Harry said, feeling her nose begin to twitch. She had momentarily forgotten about her allergy to the dog. If she sneezed, she was going to blow her brains out. "I want you to meet my partner, Judy Johnson."

"Pleased to meet you," Dan said automatically as he shook hands with Judy.

"Likewise, I'm sure," Judy said with a pleasant smile.

"Now, what can I get you to drink?" Dan asked.

"Nothing for me," Harry replied, taking a tissue out of her purse and carefully blowing her nose. Her headache flared and then subsided, but it was only a matter of time before her sinuses would become blocked. When that happened, she was going to be in serious trouble.

"Oh, come on, now," Dan protested. "I know how much you like a stiff rum and Coke."

"Doctor's orders," Harry lied, although she was certain that Nora would disapprove of her drinking. "I'll just have a glass of water."

"Well, I can't argue with Nora, can I?" Dan said amiably. "What about you, Judy?"

"The same thing," Judy told him. "I have to drive."

"Hardly anybody knows how to drink anymore," Dan joked, pouring two glasses of mineral water. "I guess I'll have to make up for the rest of you."

"Then I hope Betty is going to be driving tonight," Harry commented.

"Dad, have you seen – oh, hi, Miss Hubbley," Chip said. "How're you doing?"

"Fine, Chip," Harry replied, glancing at the young man standing in front of her. "And you?"

"Great," Chip said as he poured himself a glass of cola.

Dan glanced at his son, and said, "Are you planning to go out this evening?"

Chip shrugged and looked bored.

Harry stared at Chip and once again reflected about how familiar he looked, although he didn't resemble either Betty of Dan. "You must look like one of your grandparents," she commented casually.

"I dunno," Chip said sullenly.

"He looks like himself, I guess," Dan remarked as he poured an indeterminate amount of rum into his glass. "Genes are funny things, aren't they?"

It couldn't be! Harry thought. But if it was, what a motive for murder. "I'll be right back," she said abruptly, blowing her nose again.

"Are you all right?" Judy asked at once.

"Yes," Harry said. "I'm fine. I'm just going to the little girl's room. Too much water," she said, holding up her empty glass and then placing it on the table.

She left the room, wanting to hurry but knowing better. She felt fragile and didn't want to do anything to make her headache worse. Hurrying would do that, as would laughing or moving abruptly or turning her head too swiftly. She slowly mounted the stairs, hoping that she would find Betty on the second floor and that the puppy was in another part of the house, or better yet, outdoors. When she calculated that no one on the ground floor would be able to hear her, she called Betty's name out loud.

"Harriet? Are you looking for me?"

Harry followed Betty's voice into one of the bedrooms.

"Lord, Harriet, your head looks awful!" Betty exclaimed, coming closer to get a better look.

"It looks worse than it is," Harry said, sitting down on the edge of the bed. "Is this your room?"

"Yes," Betty replied, glancing around. "Goodness, it's a bit of a mess, isn't it?"

"Never mind," Harry said.

"I just hope you're all right. People say that Nora Hopkins is a good doctor, but we've never gone to her. I'd feel funny about having one of my childhood friends as my doctor. That's probably illogical, but there it is. Anyway, I was just getting ready for the party," Betty said, returning to the dresser. "Did you want something?"

"How old is Chip?" Marry asked, watching Betty run a brush through her hair. If only she would just tell Harry how old he was without bothering to ask why she wanted to know. If only she went on to talk about some other family matter or told Harry what the kids had been up to or what the puppy had destroyed today…

"Why on earth would you come all the way up here to ask that?"

"I'm just curious," Harry replied evasively, unwilling to verbalize her suspicions. She sniffed and searched through her purse for another tissue. Her headache was getting worse, but she couldn't leave now, not when she was this close to discovering something so important.

"He's twenty-five," Betty answered. "He should be out on his own by now, but these days, what can you do? He wasn't a good student and he flunked out of trade school. And there's certainly no chance of him getting on one of the boats. Dan tried, but there's no jobs."

"His hair is so much darker than yours or Dan's," Harry commented.

"That happens, doesn't it?" Betty replied with a nervous laugh as she opened a tube of lipstick and expertly painted her lips.

"And he's a lot taller than either of you," Harry continued. She was afraid of what it would do to her head to sniffle with any amount of vigour, so she dabbed at her nose with a tissue instead.

"Children are always taller than their parents," Betty insisted. "It's the improved nutrition. Our brood eats better than we ever did as kids, that's for sure."

"He certainly doesn't resemble you or Dan," Harry pushed. She could be wrong, she thought. She could be badgering one of her oldest friends for nothing.

"We'd better go, Harry," Betty said to her.

"He doesn't look like any of the other kids, either," Harry said, watching Betty toss her brush and lipstick into her purse.

"Don't," Betty said in a quiet voice.

"I'm on the right track, aren't I?" Harry asked, slipping her last tissue into her pants pocket and rising slowly from the bed.

"How did you know?" Betty whispered, staring at Harry in the mirror as Harry approached her from behind.

"He looks like Wayne when Wayne was young," Harry replied. "He has the same way of holding himself, the same eyes, the same hair. I didn't notice the resemblance the first time I saw him, but tonight, when he stood there and poured himself a cola, it hit me like a bolt of lightning."

"It was awful," Betty said, dropping her purse on the dresser.

"You and Wayne were lovers in high school, weren't you?" Harry asked.

"Why on earth would you think that?" Betty replied. "I was never with Wayne until after Dan and I were married."

"What?" Harry said, astonished. "But Margaret told me…"

"That Margaret Ross," Betty said scornfully. "She's the biggest gossip in Spruce Bay. Her family used to live behind mine, and I suppose she saw Wayne come over when my parents weren't home."

"That's right," Harry answered, sitting back down on the bed as Betty began to pace the floor. Her head throbbed but she didn't dare let Betty know how much pain she was in.

"I used to help him with his homework. He swore me to secrecy because he didn't want people to know he cared about his marks," Betty said.

"Margaret was certain the two of you were having an affair," Harry commented.

"He gave it his best shot, but I wasn't having any of it," Betty told her. "I was too afraid I'd get pregnant. And Wayne wasn't the most patient guy in school. He could have his choice of any number of girls, so he didn't wait around for me to change my mind. Believe it or not, I was a virgin when Dan and I got married."

"But why on earth did you get involved with Wayne later on?" Harry asked.

"I don't know how to tell you this or whether I should even mention it. Dan will kill me if he finds out I ever breathed a word of it to anyone," Betty said with a sigh.

"Why? Was Dan impotent?" Harry said, half joking, but she immediately turned serious when she saw the look on Betty's face. "Oh my lord, he was, wasn't he?" she asked, getting up and closing the door.

"No one ever knew, Harriet," Betty said. "He wouldn't go for help."

"Do you mean to tell me that…"

"Wayne was the first," Betty whispered, sitting down beside Harry. "I just couldn't stand it anymore. Dan tried, but without anyone to help us, it just got worse. He started to avoid going to bed when I did. He would stay up and fall asleep in front of the television or go out to the tavern and come home stinking of beer. Our marriage began to fall apart. We couldn't even show affection for each other anymore, so I turned to Wayne for understanding as much as sex."

Harry could picture Betty and Dan as a young small-town couple experiencing problems in their sexual relationship. Dan would have been confused and wanting to do the right thing but too macho to admit to anyone that he couldn't make love to his wife. He would have been afraid that the guys on the trawler or his hunting buddies would find out. Betty wouldn't have had anywhere to turn, either. Imagine going home to mother and saying that your husband couldn't get it up!

"I happened to run into Wayne on Main Street one day, and we went out for coffee. One thing led to another, and Chip was the result," Betty continued not looking at Harry.

Harry's last tissue disintegrated in her hand. "Have you got any tissues?"

"On the bedside table," Betty said, pointing behind her.

Harry turned too quickly, and pain blossomed throughout her head. She touched her forehead and groaned.

"Harriet Hubbley, I knew you were too sick to be up and about," Betty said instantly. "Lie down on the bed while I call your friend."

"No, I'm fine," Harry said, taking a deep breath and willing the pain away. She ignored her dripping nose, held herself perfectly still and felt her headache recede to a manageable level. "Did Wayne know about Dan's problem?"

"Of course not," Betty insisted. "Do you think I would have even considered telling him?"

"No," Harry replied. Not if Betty was in her right mind, she thought. Only a fool would have told Wayne something they wanted kept secret.

"Don't be thick-headed, Harriet," Betty responded. "How could I have hidden it from him? Or pretended that it was his child when we'd never made love? I had no choice but to tell him. You can only hide the fact that you're pregnant for so long. That was the only time he ever hit me," she said with a sigh.

"What happened then?"

"We talked about my having an abortion, but that was never a real option for either of us," Betty continued. "We decided to have the baby. And Dan's always treated Chip like his own, even when we worked through our problems and had more children."

"How did Dan feel about Wayne?"

"Do you have to ask?"

"No."

"But don't go getting any funny ideas in your head, Harriet," Betty warned as she rose from the bed. "If he had wanted to get even with Wayne, Dan would have done it then. He wouldn't have waited for so long, that's for sure. It happened twenty-five years ago, after all."

Except that Dan had raised a child who was the spitting image of Wayne Williams, Harry thought as she slowly stood up. She tried to imagine how that would make a man like Dan feel and failed. "Did Wayne every try to – to see Chip, or to, you know, come around?" Harry asked. How on earth could she ask if Wayne had been blackmailing them? That was not the kind of question you normally put to your friends.

"Why on earth would he? He didn't know the child was his," Betty answered.

"You never told him?"

"God, no! Has that bump on your head affected your brain?" Betty retorted.

"Maybe," Harry said with a short laugh. "Wayne could be pretty despicable at times, so I thought that he might have asked for money to keep things quiet."

"I can't believe I'm hearing this," Betty said with a stunned look on her face. "There was never anything like that. Never!"

"Just one more thing."

"What?"

"Does Chip know?"

"I hope you're not implying that he had something to do with Wayne's death," Betty said, her voice trembling.

"I didn't say that," Harry asserted. "I just asked if he knew."

"Of course not. We never, ever considered telling him," Betty said curtly as she left the bedroom.

"Harry?" came Judy's voice shortly after.

"Coming," Harry said dispiritedly. Buck up, she told herself. Her headache would lessen as soon as she got out of this house and away from its allergens. Now, if she could only add up the clues, subtract the obviously lies, and discover who had killed Wayne.

Chapter 19

"You were supposed to call me," Police Chief Sandy Burns said acrimoniously, cornering Harry on the deck of Linda and Mike's cottage. He was dressed in bright plaid shorts, a white shirt and a powder blue sports jacket. Next to him, Harry felt like a fashion plate.

"I knew you'd be here, so I thought I'd wait," Harry fibbed, taking a sip of water.

"Well," he said indecisively, and then she could feel him backing off. "Are you okay?"

"I thought you'd never ask," Harry couldn't resist saying.

"Aw, come on, Harriet," he complained. "Do you think this is easy?"

"Solving a murder isn't supposed to be easy," Harry replied, refusing to be congenial. "Do you mind if we sit down? My head hurts."

"By all means, let's sit down," he said hurriedly, leading her to several lawn chairs clustered around a table at the far end of the deck. "We checked out the church, but we didn't find anything but the cross. And we asked around, but no one saw anything."

"I didn't think you would," Harry said tiredly.

"Why did you go back there after the service was over, anyway?" Sandy asked.

"I left my purse in one of the pews," Harry responded.

"When I questioned you in the emergency room, you said you had no idea who hit you," he continued.

"And I still don't," Harry replied. "I didn't have time to turn around."

"And you didn't hear anything while you were in the church?" he inquired.

Harry thought for a moment, trying to remember. "Actually, I did hear something. It was a distant thud that I assumed was coming from outside. It sounded like somebody shutting a car door."

"Could it have been one of the church doors closing?" Sandy asked.

"I suppose it could have been," Harry said slowly, revising her opinion of him. Perhaps it had been a lucky guess.

"Maybe someone followed you into the church," Sandy suggested, taking a sip of beer.

"Judy," Harry called to her lover, who was standing on the edge of the patio gazing out to sea. When Judy turned to look at her, Harry motioned to her to approach them. "Did you see anybody in the church yard while you were waiting for me?"

"No," Judy replied, looking suspiciously at Sandy Burns.

"Did any cars pass by?" Sandy asked.

"I don't think so," Judy answered. "But don't forget that I couldn't see the side door Harry used or the back of the church."

"True. But it's a dead time of day, if you'll excuse the pun," Harry commented. "Everyone goes to church and then goes home for lunch."

"You're right," Chief Burns said. "So, who knew you were going back to the church to look for your purse?"

"Vivi was with us when I realized I didn't have it," Harry replied reluctantly.

"Vivi Andrews," he said with a contented smile, sitting back in his chair.

"Although it could have been anyone who went to church and noticed that I left my purse behind and that my rental car was still in the parking lot. They probably concluded that I would come back for my purse and the car at the same time," Harry reminded him.

"But most of our class was in church this morning," Sandy commented.

"Precisely," Harry replied.

"Aw, hell, it had to be one of them who killed Wayne," he said. "I don't suppose you did it, though, not after somebody gave you that bump on the head."

"Isn't that nice, Harry? He doesn't think you did it," Judy said sweetly as she crossed her arms over her chest and walked away.

"There's no need for her to act that way," Sandy griped.

Harry tried not to laugh.

"I mean, where does she get off, saying something like that to me?" he complained.

"You weren't exactly polite to her in the emergency room this morning," Harry reminded him.

He looked at Harry as if she had just kicked him in the balls. "Polite?" he yelped. "Who said I had to be polite? I'm the Chief of Police."

"That doesn't give you the licence to be nasty or overbearing or to discriminate against people," Harry told him.

"Why don't you go back where you came from? We don't want your kind around here," he said angrily.

"Speak for yourself, Sandy Burns," Harry said as she rose cautiously from the lawn chair. "But there's one thing you got right, and that's the fact that I didn't kill Wayne. But I'm not sure I can say the same thing about you."

"What are you talking about?" he shouted, rising from his chair.

"Julia and Wayne," Harry replied.

"How did you find out about that?" he replied, sitting back down. "Hell, never mind. There are enough busybodies in this town to fill the county jail. But you're talking about old news. That happened years ago, before Julia and I got married. Stuff like that doesn't mean a thing now. I mean, how could we ever figure out who killed Wayne if we have to go back that far?"

"Precisely," Harry said.

"Damnit," he muttered. He sat there and stared at her for several seconds and then shook his head and finished his beer.

Harry walked to the edge of the patio and looked out over the ocean. It was just after six and the sun wouldn't set for another couple of hours. Mike would soon turn on the barbecue and grill steaks. Eddie had asked him if they were the same ones he had been cooking Friday night, which had successfully broken the ice and made them all laugh, but her classmates were still subdued and edgy. It was impossible to forget what had happened to Wayne down on the beach two nights ago.

She looked through the patio doors and saw Dan and Betty having a heated conversation in the kitchen. Suddenly, Dan stormed out and headed directly for Harry. Well, at least Sandy Burns was easily accessible should things get out of hand, she thought nervously.

Dan stopped in front of her. "Do you think I killed Wayne?" But that wasn't what was really bothering him, Harry realized the minute she saw the sick look in his red-rimmed eyes. He hated the idea that anyone else knew about his sexual problems with his wife.

"I don't know," Harry answered honestly.

"Well, I didn't," he responded, taking a large swig of his drink.

"Under the circumstances, I find that hard to believe," Harry replied.

"You don't know what you're talking about," Dan retorted, trying to control his temper.

"I think I do," Harry responded quietly. "And don't be so angry with me, Dan."

"She shouldn't have told you," he said vehemently.

"I guessed."

"I don't care. She shouldn't have admitted it."

Harry turned away and watched a boat sail by. Two young children waved to her, so she waved back.

"I didn't kill him, Harriet," Dan said softly. She felt his hand encircle her upper arm, but she didn't pull away. "Look, I'm going to tell you something that nobody else knows now that Wayne is dead, but you've got to promise you'll never breathe a word of it to anybody. Not even Betty."

"I won't," Harry replied, feeling his hand drop away.

"I got even, all right," Dan said. "One night when I knew Wayne was in town, I went out and had a few drinks to build up my courage. Then I went looking for him and beat the shit out of him."

"You're kidding!" Harry exclaimed, realizing even as she spoke that he wasn't.

"After that, I decided to have some fun of my own," he added.

"I see," Harry said, and she did. Dan had had an affair or two himself and had likely and quite unintentionally cured himself of impotence.

"That's the way I got it out of my system," Dan explained, looking self-conscious.

"And paid Betty back," Harry added.

"Yeah, I guess so," Dan conceded, "although it sounds so mean when you put it that way. But I did what I had to do. After a while Betty and I came to terms with things and got on with our lives. No one else knows that Chip was Wayne's. Except for you."

"But Chip looks so much like Wayne," Harry commented.

"Maybe so, but Wayne never saw him," Dan replied.

"Are you sure?"

"As sure as I can be."

"What about other people? Don't you think anyone else noticed?" Harry asked.

"It's not all that unusual for some kids to look really different from the parents," Dan responded.

"I suppose not."

"Once in a while somebody says something, but we just laugh it off. And there's another thing," Dan said. "Betty told me that you asked whether Wayne was blackmailing us because of what happened. I've never heard of such a stupid thing in my life. I fish for a living, and you know what that's like these days. We've got eight kids, and Betty doesn't work. What the hell do you think he was blackmailing us for?"

Good question, Harry thought.

"I didn't kill Wayne," he said softly.

Harry believed him. His life hadn't been easy. His wife had become pregnant by another man, and he had raised the child. He had been forced to struggle to make a living from the increasingly inhospitable North Atlantic and he probably knew that, financially, things weren't going to get any better.

"Anyway, I told Betty I'd be back in a minute," he said gruffly.

"I'm glad we talked about this," Harry said, turning to him.

"I'm not. So just forget about it, will you?" he responded, walking away without looking at her.

Harry glanced at Mike, who had just come out of the kitchen carrying a platter piled high with steaks. He walked over to the barbecue, put the platter on a side table and bent down to put several on the grill, which was already hot.

"So, Mike – Michael – here I am again," Harry announced. "Need some help?"

"Oh, go ahead and call me Mike," he said. "It doesn't matter."

"You sound depressed," Harry remarked.

"I just wish this would all end," Mike said, rearranging the steaks with a barbeque fork so the last one would fit on the grill. "Wayne being murdered down there," he said, using his fork to point toward the beach, "you attacked in my church – you might have been killed, too."

"I'm okay," Harry said. And she did feel better. Her allergies had dispersed, and her headache had retreated the moment she left Dan and Betty's house. Her head hurt, but she could concentrate.

"You can't believe how relieved I feel," he responded. "I just hope nothing happens to anyone else."

"You and me both," Harry responded fervently.

"Would you pass me the barbecue sauce, please?" he asked. "It's on the table."

Harry picked up a bowl containing thick tomato sauce and handed it to him. "Homemade?"

"Yes," he replied. "I cook up a big batch every summer."

"I can't wait to taste it," Harry commented. "Mike, can I ask you something?"

"Is it going to be as rude as what you asked me this morning?" he inquired with a grin.

"Heaven forbid!" Harry said with mock horror. "I don't think I could stand another battle like that."

"Me neither," Mike replied. "That's why I wanted to know." He used the fork to turn the steaks over and then brushed sauce on each of them. "Okay, shoot."

"Who do you think might have had a reason to kill Wayne?"

"The answer is no; I didn't do it," Mike replied.

"That's not what I asked," Harry protested.

"But that's what you mean," he returned. "Look, I'm as smart as the next person, and it's perfectly evident that it had to be one of us. That's the only logical solution."

"That's why I asked what you thought," Harry insisted. "You know all these people, after all."

Mike studied her for a moment and then turned and flipped some steaks. "Do you realize what it would do to my reputation if I burned these?"

"They'd fire you, right?" Harry responded. "I mean, any pastor who couldn't barbeque a decent steak couldn't possibly preach a good sermon."

"You're too swift for me, Harriet," Mike said with a grin.

"And you're very adept at changing the subject," Harry told him.

"I didn't kill him," Mike said after he glanced around to confirm that they were alone. "He was one of the most despicable people I have ever met, he was having an affair with my wife, but I didn't lay a finger on him."

"You know?"

"Linda thinks she's so discreet," Mike interrupted, an implausibly fond smile flitting across his face. "But the truth is, she's about as subtle as a bull charging a red flag. One part of her wants to keep it secret, but another part wants to flaunt it."

"You don't care about what she does?" Harry asked sceptically.

"Not as long as my parishioners don't find out," Mike replied as he lowered the heat on the barbecue and turned some of the steaks over. "Most people – Protestants, anyway, I can't speak for other faiths – are religious before they decide to become ministers. They marry other religious people. But I wasn't religious at all, and when Linda and I married, we were perfected suited to each other. Then I changed completely. But you can't order people to get religion. It doesn't happen that way."

"I suppose not," Harry responded.

"The only thing I could do was to ask her to keep things quiet."

Harry was confused. She stood and watched Mike brush more barbecue sauce on the steaks, which were sizzling and emitting a tantalizing aroma. He knew about Linda's lovers, about Wayne, but he didn't care. Correct that: he knew, but he cared solely about Linda keeping her affairs quiet. Since Harry found it difficult to accept Judy's relationship with another woman, she could hardly imagine a man being so tolerant. Maybe he wasn't telling the truth.

"You don't understand, do you?"

"Well, it is rather unusual," Harry said.

"Not if you accept the fact that Linda and I are no longer in love with each other," Mike said in a composed voice. "Do you know how difficult it is for a minister to get divorced? Oh, the United Church bureaucracy says all kinds of liberal things about divorce and, in fact, homosexuality, as you probably know, since there's been a lot in the media about it in the past few years. But my career would go right down the tubes if Linda and I got divorced. And do you know why?" he asked rhetorically.

"Because people in towns like this don't want a minister who's divorced, no matter what the church says about it."

"Then you have a marriage of convenience," Harry said.

"Precisely."

"And Wayne didn't try to blackmail you?" Harry asked abruptly.

"What?" he yelped, nearly dropping the barbecue fork. "You've got to be kidding!"

"He could have ruined you."

"You've got an incredibly suspicious mind," he said, glancing at her. "But nothing like that happened."

"Perhaps he was blackmailing Linda," Harry suggested.

"Where would she get the money?"

"She has a job."

"For which she is paid a little over minimum wage," he replied. "That would hardly make blackmail worthwhile, would it?"

"I suppose not," Harry admitted.

"Anyway, I would have known about it. Linda can't keep a secret for very long," he said, turning back to the barbecue.

So that was that, Harry though as she watched him brush on more barbecue sauce.

"Darling," Linda said as she joined them, giving Harry a gentle hug. "I heard what happened to you. And look at that dreadful cut on your head. Couldn't you at least get rid of the blood? Or aren't you allowed to shower for an impossibly long period of time? Are you sure you should be standing up? Let me bring you a nice, strong drink to calm your nerves. I know I needed one when Dan told me."

"I'm doing just fine," Harry replied. "And I can't drink anything alcoholic as long as I have a headache. I wouldn't mind another glass of water, but I'm going in for a bit, so I'll get it."

"Are you sure? Don't overexert yourself," Linda urged.

"I won't."

"By the way, your friend is quite nice," Linda said.

"Oh, you mean my lover Judy?" Harry answered. "Yes, she's very nice." Harry smiled at them and walked back to the cottage.

"Well?" July asked when they met in the kitchen.

"I need another glass of water." Harry opened the freezer door, took out several ice cubes and tossed them into her glass.

"Come on, Harry, did you find out anything?" Judy asked impatiently, putting her arm around Harry's waist.

"I don't know if it's safe to talk here," Harry responded cautiously as she leaned against her lover.

"But there's no one around."

"There's bound to be someone around," Harry insisted, and, sure enough, seconds later Teresa walked into the kitchen.

Harry glanced at Judy and then at Teresa, but she didn't move away from her lover.

"We've already met," Judy said tonelessly, leaving Harry with no doubt about the tenor of their conversation.

Teresa walked past as if she hadn't seen them.

"Phew!" Harry exclaimed.

"You'd better believe it," Judy said with feeling. "For a minute there, I thought she was going to stop. Are you sure that she didn't kill him?"

"Being a born-again Christian doesn't predispose people to commit murder," Harry replied.

"I suppose not," Judy said. "Too bad, though. That is one strange lady."

"Who's one strange lady," Eddie asked as he and Margaret strolled hand-in-hand into the kitchen.

"Eddie, where are your manners?" Margaret scolded her fiancé before she turned to Harry. "Are you all right, Harriet? We heard all about your unfortunate mishap."

"I'm fine," Harry replied. "Recovering nicely."

"Who's one strange lady? Someone we know?" Eddie asked again.

"Teresa," Harry said.

"That's old news," Margaret said, sounding disappointing.

"Not to me. Don't forget, until this weekend I hadn't seen her since we graduated," Harry reminded her.

"It must have been quite a shock," Margaret said.

"It's not only her, Margie," Eddie maintained. "Look at us – why, Harriet didn't even recognize us Friday night."

"That's true," Margaret agreed. "Well, thirty years is a long time."

"So, who do the two of you think killed Wayne?" Harry asked, opening the fridge and taking out a large bottle of water.

Margaret and Eddie looked at each other and then at Harry.

"Well?" Harry asked, filling her water glass and drinking half of it.

"Oh, they probably think it was me," Vivi said casually as she breezed into the kitchen. She was wearing a revealing cross-over white blouse tied at the waist and skin-tight western jeans and she looked like a million dollars. "What is that, Harriet, water? Good, it'll go quite well with my scotch."

"Dinner's ready," Linda popped in to announce.

"Great," Eddie said, taking Margaret's hand. "Let's go."

"I'll meet you outside," Harry said to Judy.

"Sure," Judy replied. "But don't let your steak get cold."

"You've been making yourself scarce," Harry commented once she and Vivi were alone in the kitchen.

"Once she arrived, I didn't think there was much point in hanging around," Vivi said. "Aren't you going to offer me some water?"

Harry filled her glass. "You've never been the type to hang around," Harry commented.

"You're quite right, Harriet. You've become quite astute, haven't you?" Vivi replied, sipping her scotch and water. "But don't think I'm jealous. I'm not the type. It's just that if nothing's happening in one place, I move on to another."

"Tell me about you and Wayne," Harry asked, although what she really wanted to know was why Vivi was ignoring the bloody spot on the side of her head. Or why she hadn't volunteered information about what type of place she had moved on to. Or, realistically speaking, who she had moved on to. She suddenly wished she could have a drink. It wasn't easy to expel from her mind the importance Vivi had played in her early life. Or to banish the desire she had felt and her foolish fantasies that Vivi would reciprocate it.

"I told you about that," Vivi said complacently.

"Not everything," Harry asserted.

"How on earth can you tell?" Vivi asked, sounding genuinely interested.

"I know you too well," Harry responded.

"Naw, you're just guessing," Vivi said. "Nobody really knows me."

"Have it your own way, then," Harry replied, crossing her arms.

"I could tell you something that no one else knows," Viv teased in a low, confidential voice.

"What?" Harry asked expectantly.

"Not here, dummy," Vivi retorted, sounding amused.

"Let's go outside, then," Harry suggested.

"Great idea. I'm starving," Vivi said.

"That's not what I meant, and you know it," Harry remonstrated.

"If I don't demolish one of those steaks within the next five minutes, I'm going to faint from hunger," Vivi said with a laugh. "So come on."

Harry picked up the bottle of water and followed Vivi from the kitchen. "Tell me," she urged.

"You are so darn persistent," Vivi chuckled. "Why don't you guess?"

Guess? How could she possibly guess? "You know damn well that I can't do that," Harry replied. "Why don't you give me a hint? Or just tell me. Frankly, I'm too tired to play guessing games. My head hurts like hell and I need something to eat."

"Darling, I can't think when I'm this hungry," Vivi announced. "I'll tell you what – meet me out front later."

"When?" Harry asked.

"Later," Vivi said impatiently. "After dinner."

"Where?" Harry asked.

"Harry! Come eat," Judy called.

"Oh, lord, I've forgotten my drink," Vivi remarked, turning back to the house.

Harry walked to the patio and joined Judy at one of the picnic tables, certain that Viv was playing with her. She could wait in front of the cottage all night and Vivi wouldn't show up. So, she wouldn't go. Let Vivi tease someone else, not her.

Chapter 20

Harry speared another hunk of steak, raised it to her mouth, and then reconsidered and put it back on her plate. She'd had enough. She had managed to eat half of the thick, juicy steak Judy had placed on her plate, but she couldn't swallow another bite. Her headache had grown worse again, and all she wanted was to go back to the motel, lie down and forget about this nightmare and where her thoughts were leading her.

So many of her former classmates had motives to kill Wayne. He had taken Betty's virginity and fathered her first child after she was already married to Dan. He had maintained an ongoing liaison with Linda both before and after she had married Mike. Dan and Mike had grounds to kill him, especially if Wayne had taunted them about his relationships with their wives, and Harry wouldn't have put past him to do just that. Sandy Burns might have had the same motive except that Harry hadn't uncovered any evidence to link his wife to Wayne once they had graduated from high school.

And what about the women? Linda probably had the strongest motive, since she had been in a relationship with Wayne up until the time of his death. Betty hadn't been involved with him for a long time, although Harry supposed that bearing and raising his child could probably be considered some form of involvement.

Both couples denied having been blackmailed, and she tended to believe them. Neither of them had much money. Mike and Linda were probably better off, as both were working, and they didn't have children. Ministers didn't make much, although they earned more than fishers. Of course, Wayne could have been bleeding them over a long period of time, taking a little from one, a little from the other. And perhaps there were others – like Vivi…

"Full?" Judy asked, pushing her plate away. She had demolished her steak, two baked potatoes topped with sour cream and chives, several pieces of garlic bread and a bowl of salad.

"Completely," Harry said with a sigh.

"How are you feeling?"

"Lousy," Harry admitted. "My head hurts like hell."

"We should probably leave soon."

"You're right," Harry agreed, "but not just yet. Have you seen Vivi? She promised to tell me something after dinner."

"She's holding court over there," Judy replied, pointing toward the end of the patio where several of Harry's classmates were seated around another picnic table.

"You don't like her very much, do you?" Harry remarked, looking out to sea. The sun was setting over the water, but the sunset was disappointing because there weren't many clouds in the sky to reflect the crimson light.

"We've been through this before," Judy replied wearily. "It doesn't matter whether I like her or not. You would, of course, feel guilty if you didn't like one of my lovers. But I'm not obligated to choose someone you like, and you're not required to like whom I choose."

"Fine," Harry said, rising from the picnic table. She was so utterly exhausted that she couldn't deal with this tonight, if ever. "To tell the truth, I don't much like Vivi myself. I'm going in for another bottle of mineral water. I'll be back in a couple of minutes."

"I'll get it," Judy offered. "You look bushed."

"Don't bother," Harry responded. "I have to go to the bathroom anyway."

Harry could feel her lover's eyes on her back, but she didn't turn around. Being in a relationship was hard sometimes, especially when it was with a woman who never stopped searching for the truth. Her own unique truth, perhaps, but one which sometimes forced Harry to deal with issues which weren't her own. On the other hand, maybe she was lazy. Perhaps Judy was right to believe that people were alive to test the boundaries, not to sit on their butts and bask in conformity.

She walked from the kitchen into the living room. Everyone was outside eating, so the house was deserted, and she didn't have to wait to use the bathroom. She decided to avoid looking in the mirror, but curiosity got the better of her and she glanced in it as she was leaving. That was a mistake. She stopped, her feet rooted to the spot, her eyes riveted to the reflection. She looked so awful that she immediately felt worse.

"I thought I told you to rest," a voice said reproachfully.

Harry started and her headache flared. She hadn't heard Nora come in.

"Just look at you," Nora grumbled, walking into the bathroom and gently grasping Harry's head in her hands. "You're as pale as a ghost and you have two black eyes in which I read extreme agony and near exhaustion."

"I'm not doing anything strenuous," Harry said defensively.

"Just being on your feet is arduous when you've had the kind of bump on the head that you're had," Norma said, releasing her. "Why don't you ask your lover to take you home?"

Home. How she wished she could go home to Montreal, crawl into her own bed with its familiar sheets and comforting smells and her very own pillow which didn't leave her with a stiff neck in the morning.

"You look like you're going to cry," Nora said, sounding surprised. She reached behind her, closed the door and then put the lid down on the toilet seat. "Why don't you sit down?"

"I'm all right," Harry said. "It's just that sometimes things feel a bit overwhelming."

"Sit!" Nora insisted.

Harry did, although she hated sitting on toilet seats. She always felt like they were going to collapse from her weight. This one slid sideways and then stabilized.

"Promise me you'll rest," Nora said.

"I will."

"I'm glad I ran into you," Nora said, filling a plastic water glass and handing it to Harry. "I was going to call you tomorrow if you didn't come tonight, although I somehow suspected you'd be here."

"To see how I was doing?" Harry asked, sipping the water.

Nora looked like she wanted to pace, but there wasn't room. She leaned against the door and studied Harry.

"What?" Harry asked. Even though her health was good, she always got nervous when a doctor stared at her like that.

"Did Sandy Burns tell you anything about Wayne's state of health when he died?" Nora asked.

"It didn't come up," Harry answered. "Why?"

"He had AIDS," Nora said, her gaze shifting to a spot a couple of inches over Harry's head.

Harry jumped to her feet and nearly collapsed from the pain.

"Sorry," Nora said, grasping Harry under the arms to prevent her from falling. "There's no easy way to tell someone something like that. Now, sit down and stay there."

Harry closed her eyes and leaned against the toilet tank. She shouldn't have been surprised that Wayne had AIDS. She had seen that gaunt look so many times before as gay male friends of hers had sickened and died, especially before the drug cocktails had been introduced. Given that HIV was well on its way to becoming a chronic disease, she hadn't expected to see it in the face of a former classmate, so she hadn't recognized it. "How did you find out? From the autopsy?"

"No, from his doctor in Toronto." Nora replied.

"Are you sure?"

"Yes," Nora answered firmly. "And that's why I wanted to talk to you."

"To me?" Harry said, opening her eyes.

"Did you and Vivi practice safer sex?" Nora asked.

Oh my god, Harry thought with dismay. "Vivi isn't sick, is she?" And anyway, how did Nora know she and Vivi had made love?

"I don't know."

"But you think she might be?"

"If she had unprotected sex with Wayne, she was at risk," Nora concurred. "But right now, I'm concerned about you."

"We used gloves," Harry said quietly.

"What about oral sex?"

"We didn't do that."

"Good."

"She didn't even kiss me," Harry said. "But there's still a chance, isn't there?"

"Probably not," Nora responded. "But you should ask Vivi if she's HIV positive, and if she is, you should think about having a test now and again in six months. And you should practice safer sex until you're sure you're not infected."

"AIDS tests?" Harry asked breathlessly. How could this be happening to her?

"Look, you're probably okay," Nora said. "But you should be cautious."

"That's the doctor speaking, Harry said. "What about the lesbian?"

"The lesbian isn't particularly worried," Nora admitted with a wry smile, "although she's going to get tested just to be certain."

Of course. Nora had also slept with Vivi. That's how she knew that Harry had, too. If Vivi had been true to form, she would have bragged about bedding Harry. "Thanks for telling me," Harry said.

"I felt I had to," Nora replied. "Otherwise, you might never have known. Wayne's family has asked the police and the medical examiner to keep it quiet, if possible."

Harry looked at Nora, her thoughts coming fast and furious. "That could have been why he was murdered."

"That occurred to me too," Nora responded. "But I'm a doctor, not a cop."

"Why didn't Wayne start taking meds as soon as he was diagnosed with HIV?" Harry mused. "He might never have ended up with AIDS."

"I know," Nora replied. "Only Wayne could answer that question, and he's no longer able to."

Someone knocked on the door.

"I hope that's not Teresa," Harry muttered as she slowly rose to her feet.

Nora snorted and opened the door.

It was Vivi. "Well, well, ladies, fancy meeting you here," she said, her voice dripping with innuendo. "Shame on you, Nora, conducting a physical in such a vulgar place."

"Still jumping to conclusions, I see," Nora responded with a chuckle as she sauntered off.

"What's this secret you've been promising to tell me?" Harry asked, although she was now practically certain she knew.

"Let's meet down on the beach in a couple of minutes," Vivi said with a mysterious smile. "I've got to use the facilities first," she added, strolling into the bathroom and closing the door behind her.

"Fine," Harry murmured to herself. She left the house and walked through the copse of trees, wishing she could hurry but not wanting her headache to flare. She was certain that someone had been watching her when she had strolled through the woods on Friday evening, but she didn't hear any strange noises now, or sense any hostile presence, or a friendly one, for

that matter. And she certainly wasn't going to stop and wait for
something to happen.

She soon came to the beach. It was a beautiful evening.
The moon was nearly full, the sky cloudless and the surface of
the ocean rippled continuously, leading Harry to believe there
was a powerful riptide not far from shore, which would make it
dangerous to swim. Waves slapped lazily against the beach, and
far off in the distance she could hear the foghorn bleating. She
walked across the sand to the end of the dock and sat down,
letting her feet hang over the edge.

She loved the coast, the ocean, the smells associated
with the sea, but she was too distressed to enjoy them. She had
been battling her thoughts all day, attempting to dismiss her
increasingly strong suspicions about Vivi, but she couldn't
combat them any longer. She had wondered whether Wayne was
blackmailing Vivi with the threat of telling her second husband
about their affair, but that was before she had learned that Wayne
had AIDS. What if Vivi was HIV positive? Would she have
killed for revenge? But Linda could have the same motive. She
could also have infected Mike, not to mention other lovers. The
chain of sexual deceit could have been tragically long in this
instance, she thought.

"Harriet?"

"I'm out here." Harry turned and watched Vivi walk
toward her. The tide was rising, and the crest of a wave nibbled
at her toes. The water was chilly, but she didn't move her feet.

"I'm going to tell you something which no one else
knows except for my doctor," Vivi said. "I'm HIV positive."

Harry could feel the planks of the dock vibrate beneath
her as Vivi paced. "Did you contract it from Wayne?"

"It would seem so," Vivi responded. "But how did you
know about him? Did he tell you?"

"No, Nora did. When you found out, you killed him,
didn't you?" Harry asked with a sigh, forgetting about her
headache for the first time that evening.

The pacing stopped and for a long time Harry's couldn't
hear anything but the lapping of the waves against the dock. She
wondered what Vivi was doing. Thinking it over, maybe. Or
looking for shooting stars. Or preparing to kill her. She turned
abruptly and started to rise, and if Vivi hadn't grasped her, she
would have fallen into the water.

"Be careful," Vivi admonished as she released Harry and sat down beside her.

Harry's head pounded and her mouth was dry. She had thought that Vivi was going to attack her.

"I remember one summer when I was about ten or eleven," Vivi said leaning her head lightly on Harrys' shoulder. "It was the day after we finished school, and I woke up early. Everyone else was still asleep, so I got dressed and went outside. It was quiet as the grave. I sat on the swing in my back yard and swung back and forth, higher and higher until I thought I was going to flip over. As I was swinging, I felt this incredible sense of destiny. Time was infinitely expandable. It was as if every door in the world was open, and I could pass through any one of them I liked. It was like an epiphany. Have you ever experienced anything like that?"

"No," Harry replied.

"Well, fat lot of good it did, anyway," Vivi said with a self-deprecatory smile. "Just look at me now."

"How did Wayne contract AIDS?" Harry asked. The water had covered her feet, wetting the bandage covering the cut on her foot. The salt made it sting, but the chill of the water felt good. She wished she could soak her head in it.

"Drugs, most likely. I don't think I don't think he was ever addicted, but he dabbled. He told me he would try anything once, and I believed him," Vivi responded as she removed her head from Harry's shoulder.

"He looked so wasted," Harry remarked. "Why wasn't he taking the new cocktail drugs that have been so successful at preventing HIV from seroconverting to AIDS?"

"I don't know," Vivi said with a shrug. "Maybe he thought he was invincible. Or he didn't care anymore. I didn't ask, and he didn't tell me."

"Why did you kill him?" Harry asked.

"I didn't mean to," Vivi whispered, turning to face Harry. "Look, it may sound absurd coming from me, but he was completely amoral. It was like he was empty inside. Life was a series of opportunities, and people were there to be used. He didn't care about anything or anyone. Even himself."

Harry stared at her and saw that there were tears in Vivi's eyes, although it could have been the reflection of the moonlight on the waves. "What happened?"

"I found out I was HIV positive just before I flew down for the reunion," Vivi explained. "I'd suspected, but for a long time I didn't have the courage to be tested. At first, I wasn't going to come to the reunion, but then I realized that if I cancelled my trip, my husband would want to know why. Anyway, I needed some time to figure out what I was going to do. I didn't know for sure that Wayne was the one who had infected me, but he had lost so much weight and looked so awful that it wasn't hard to put two and two together. I wasn't sure whether he was going to be here, but when you said he was, I decided to have it out with him. You can't believe how angry I was. He gave me HIV, Harriet. I know it's not necessarily a death sentence anymore, but it's certainly a life-changer for someone like me. How can I hide it from my husband? He will divorce me in a minute if he finds out, so how can I take medication without him noticing? He doesn't watch me like a hawk, so I've kept him from finding out the worst things I've done in the past. And how could I suddenly ask him to start using condoms? Wayne ruined my life! And when you left me in the living room Friday night and wandered off to make coffee, I knew you wouldn't be coming back any time soon."

"You weren't as drunk as you made out to be, were you?" Harry asked.

"I wasn't drunk at all," Vivi admitted with a fleeting smile. "As soon as you went into the kitchen, I ran through the woods to the beach. He was sitting on the dock, much as we are now. We fought. He admitted he had AIDS but denied passing the virus on to me. He reminded me that he had always used a condom."

"Had he?" Harry inquired.

"Yes," Vivi responded. "In the beginning, so I wouldn't get pregnant. But before AIDS, we'd sometimes forget. Then I'd worry for a while, but there was always abortion, wasn't there? Once the AIDS scare began, I made sure all my lovers used a condom every single time. But listen to me, will you? The truth is, Harriet, that for all my posing, there haven't been that many men in my life. I talk a good line, I flirt a lot, but it often doesn't go any further than that. But, for God's sake, don't tell anyone! I wouldn't want my reputation to be in shreds, now, would I?"

"No," Harry murmured sadly.

"Of course, the problem with HIV is that it was around long before anybody knew it, so maybe we didn't start using condoms early enough," Vivi continued.

Harry bit her upper lip.

"I insulted Wayne, I berated him, I did everything I could to make him lose his temper," Vivi continued. "I wanted him to be angry so I could be angry. I wanted him to say horrible things to me. I wanted to be able to hate him. But he wouldn't play my game. He just kept smiling and that made me crazy, so I picked up a piece of wood and hit him with it."

"And that's when he fell into the water?"

"No," Vivi answered. "He fell on the dock. I was horrified, scared out of my wits, so I ran up the beach, through the trees and back into the house."

"You mean that wasn't when you pretended to find him?" Harry asked, puzzled.

"No," Vivi replied. "You must understand how I felt, Harriet. I was simply beside myself. All I could think about was getting away from his body. I hadn't meant to kill him, after all."

"And then what?"

"I had a drink and tried to calm down, Vivi said. "And then I went back to the beach and 'discovered' his body."

"Weren't you surprised that he was in the water?"

"Yes," Vivi responded, her voice trembling. "But what could I do? I thought perhaps it had rolled off the deck after I left."

"Maybe," Harry replied, thinking hard despite her headache. What would cause dead weight to move? Perhaps the sea had washed over the dock and taken Wayne's body with it. But the tide was quite high now, and the water level was nowhere near the top of the dock. The only other solution was that human hands had propelled Wayne's body into the water. But why?

"So how much of a head start are you going to give me?" Vivi asked, rising from the dock.

"None at all," Harry replied instantly. "You should give yourself up to the police, Vivi. It's no good to run. You killed Wayne, and then you attacked me in the church."

"I didn't do that, Harriet," Vivi said. "Please believe that I could never do something like that to you."

What troubled Harry was that she believed Vivi. But was her belief in Vivi because Vivi was telling the truth or because she couldn't admit to herself that a lover would hurt her physically? Was she astute or a fool?

"You owe me something, Harriet," Vivi told her. "What about our relationship?"

"What relationship?" Harry asked angrily. "If you really cared about me, you wouldn't have had sex with me. What if I've contracted HIV from you?"

"Don't be like that," Vivi appealed to Harry. "I took every precaution I could. But sex is always risky, no matter who you have it with. You should know that. And I would like to think we could part as friends," she added, extending her hand.

"I can't," Harry muttered, but her arm rose of its own volition.

"Of course you can," Vivi murmured as she grasped Harry's outstretched hand for a brief second.

Oh, lord, Harry thought as Vivi walked swiftly toward shore. She watched her cross the sand and disappear into the copse of trees between the beach and the cottage. She knew she should find Sandy Burns and tell him what she had just learned. She should, but she didn't. Something was holding her back. Her headache, perhaps. Or maybe it was her sense of loyalty, misplaced as it was. Or the feeling that something was wrong.

The water was up to her ankles and her feet felt numb. As she sat on the edge of the dock, the wind picked up and the fog poured from the sea onto the land. The moon disappeared, and with it her ability to see. Seconds later she felt the deck planks quiver and knew that someone had stepped onto the dock and was coming toward her. Had Vivi returned?

"Who is it?"

There was no reply. The deck planks stopped vibrating.

"Vivi?" Harry shouted, slipping off the edge of the dock as silently as she could. The water was breast-high and shockingly cold, but she ignored it and slid under the dock. Which one of them was it? Dan? Linda? Betty?

She moved further under the dock. It was Mike, she thought hesitantly as she listened to the footsteps overhead, loud now that she was directly under them. Or Linda, she mused indecisively. Linda was the only other woman who was still sexually involved with Wayne. Betty's liaison with him had ended decades ago, long before the age of AIDS.

The footsteps stopped again. She held her breath and tried to control her shivering even though she knew that no one could hear her over the plaintive wail of the foghorn and the sound of the waves as they restlessly wrapped themselves around the dock. The silence was suddenly knifed by a splash, and she moved laboriously through the water, cursing its resistance.

"You couldn't leave it alone, could you, Harriet?" Mike's disembodied voice came through the fog.

"You killed Wayne, didn't you?" Harriet said through chattering teeth, keeping her voice low in the hope that the fog would distort it and not give away her position. "You were on the beach, and you saw Vivi hit Wayne with a piece of wood. He was only stunned, but she didn't know that. She thought she'd killed him. You hid and waited until she left, and then you went down to the dock. Before he could recover, you used the same piece of wood to kill him. Then you dumped his body in the water, hoping it wouldn't be found until much later. Or maybe you thought that it would drift out to sea and not be found for days. But you forgot the tide was coming in, and Wayne's body stayed close to shore."

"You're too smart for your own good," Mike growled.

"Why did you do it?" Harry asked.

"I heard them fighting. I heard him tell Vivi that he had AIDS. The bastard laughed at her when she said she had tested HIV positive. He laughed, Harriet! He didn't give a damn about her," Mike responded. "And what if he gave the virus to Linda? How would it look for a minister to have an HIV-positive wife? What if she passed it on to me? He should have stopped having sex when he found out he was sick, but he had no sense of decency, no sense of responsibility toward other people. I'm glad I killed him. He deserved to die."

He sounded as if he was getting closer, so Harry reluctantly released her grip on the wharf and backed into even thicker fog, trying not to make any unnecessary noises.

"I tried to warn you," Mike said, his voice taut with repressed anger.

Suddenly Harry's feet no longer touched bottom, and her head momentarily submerged. She fought the swift-running undertow and resurfaced at once, spitting salt water. Her head was pounding but she ignored it; she knew she had no time to waste. Mike had most certainly heard her struggling. She took a step forward, but still couldn't find the bottom. She turned and tried in the other direction, but the results were the same. She treaded water, her muscles stiffening from the cold.

"It was so easy to spook you in the woods Friday night. And when you started asking all those questions, I gave you a little tap on the head in the church just to let you know that your curiosity wasn't appreciated. And to pay you back for talking to me like you did in the car that morning, for acting like I was some sort of aberration when it's people like you who are aberrant. But you just can't take a hint, can you? I'm going to have to kill you, and it's all your fault," Mike growled.

The fog had disoriented her; she no longer knew where the shore was. If she went in the wrong direction, she would soon flounder and drown in the strong current, for she had been weakened by the cold and her head wound. Where was Mike? Beside her or between her and the shore?

"Nobody knows you're here, so go right ahead and drown," Mike said with an abrupt laugh. "It would be simpler that way." His voice sounded closer, prompting Harry to make up her mind. She rose in the water and began to swim, ignoring the eruption of pain. At any moment she expected to bump into him or to feel an arm close around her throat or a hand push her under the water and hold her there until she died, but nothing happened. She swam through thick fog until one of her knees scraped a rock. She gasped with relief, let her body go limp and listened carefully, but she could hear nothing but the waves and the foghorn. She gritted her teeth, rose on her hands and knees, and pushed herself to her feet.

He could still catch her, she thought as she made her way across the beach. She tried to go faster but nearly fell. She could see the lights of the cottage through the woods but was afraid to enter the trees. She could call for help, but Mike might be lurking in the fog, ready to pounce the second she made her presence known.

In the end, she gathered the remainder of her reserves and lurched from tree to tree until she reached the front door. She fell against it, pounding with one fist and then the other until it opened and she fell into Judy's arms.

Chapter 21

"Give her some space," Nora ordered, pushing everyone aside.

"It was Mike!" Harry exclaimed as she staggered into the living room, her clothes dripping on the hardwood floor. "He killed Wayne and he just tried to kill me."

"Don't be silly," Linda protested, backing away from Harry. "He couldn't possibly have done something like that, he just went out for a minute to close the barbecue so the racoons wouldn't get in it."

"Where is he, then?" Sandy Burns interrupted, rising swiftly from an easy chair.

"In the water somewhere," Harry replied. "He was chasing me."

"Christ," Judy muttered.

"Dan, come with me," Sandy ordered. "And grab that flashlight."

"You're shivering," Judy said as Sandy and Dan rushed out.

"Let's get you out of those wet clothes," Nora said, leading her to the small, ground-floor bedroom just off the bathroom, Judy following closely behind.

"Shouldn't you be looking after Linda?" Harry muttered.

"In a minute," Nora replied brusquely. "Now shut up and sit down on that bed. Before you change, I want to have a look at your head and see what damage you've done to yourself this time."

Harry sat.

"Well, the staples are holding fine, and I don't imagine the salt water is too much of a problem, but it should still be disinfected," Nora murmured, mostly to herself. "How do you feel?"

"My head hurts," Harry responded feeling like a broken record.

"Undoubtedly," Nora replied. "And I imagine that it will continue to hurt for a couple of days yet."

"Wonderful," Harry grunted.

"Then it wasn't Vivi," Judy said.

"Well, yes and no,' Harry responded. "Vivi gave him a whack on the head with a piece of wood, which must have knocked him out. That's then Mike finished him off."

"Then where's Vivi?" Nora asked.

"Gone," Harry replied. "She thought she'd killed him, so she decided to run rather than give herself up."

"Will that woman never learn to get things right?" Nora said with real exasperation as she left the room.

Judy took Harry in her arms. "I thought you were still outside talking to Vivi. I didn't start to get worried until the fog came in and you still weren't back."

"I thought I was going to die," Harry muttered, kissing Judy on the cheek.

"You'll never know how thankful I am that you didn't," Judy replied fervently.

"Tell me," Harry whispered, holding her tight.

"Don't tease me at a time like this."

"I'm not teasing," Harry replied. "Tell me."

"I love you," Judy whispered.

Harry kissed her.

"Even your lips are cold," Judy broke off to comment. "And you're shivering. Take off those wet clothes this very minute."

They separated and Harry removed her sodden vest, T-shirt and jeans. "What am I going to wear?" she asked, drying herself with a towel.

"I'll see what's in the closet,' Judy said. "What about this?"

"That?" Harry exclaimed, looking at the frilly housecoat her lover was holding.

"It's better than running around buck naked," Judy replied dryly.

"Not by much," Harry grumbled, putting on the housecoat.

The door opened and Sandy Burns barged into the room. "Can I come in?" he asked belatedly. The legs of his pants were wet, and he looked winded.

"Why bother to ask now that you're already here?" Judy answered.

"We caught Mike," Sandy reported. "He wasn't on the beach or the dock, so we took the boat out and found him swimming around in circles. He got disoriented in the fog and couldn't find his way back to shore."

"It's a good thing you went out to look for him," Harry said. "He could have drowned in that riptide."

"He might not be so glad to be alive after we're finished with him," Sandy blustered. "Well, I've got to go. I have to drive Mike to the country jail. And Nora's going to take Linda back to the manse in her car."

"You might say thanks," Harry said, crossing her arms.

"What?" Sandy asked, looking puzzled for a moment. "Oh yeah. Well, thanks."

"You're welcome," Harry said sarcastically.

"You must have been one happy camper with him in your class," Judy commented after Sandy had gone out and closed the door.

"You can't imagine."

"I'm not even going to try. If you're up to it, I think we should return to the living room to be with the others," Judy suggested.

"Sure. I can rest just as well on a sofa as I can in bed," Harry replied. She grimaced with distaste at the frilly housecoat she was wearing and took a blanket and wrapped it around her like a sari.

"Harry! Are you all right?" Betty asked the moment they entered the living room.

"I'm fine," Harry responded heartily. "Dan, Teresa, would you mind relinquishing the sofa?"

"Of course not," Dan replied. "You must be exhausted."

"Thanks," Harry said, sitting down and arranging the blanket to cover herself from neck to toes. She felt like she would never be warm again, that even her blood was chilled.

"I can't believe that Mike killed Wayne," Margaret said suddenly.

"Mike was extremely angry with him," Harry said.

"But why?" Eddie asked. "I don't understand it."

"It's very complicated," Harry responded. "First of all, Wayne had AIDS."

"My god!" Dan exclaimed, looking at his wife.

"We don't know when he contracted it, but it was probably within the last decade. Fifteen years at the outside," Harry said, wanting to reassure Betty and Dan. "Although anyone who has been involved with Wayne should probably take the precaution of having an HIV test. I bet Halifax has a clinic which does anonymous testing.”

“Yes, yes, and then what happened?” Margaret asked impatiently.

“Unfortunately, Wayne transmitted the virus to Vivi,” Harry replied. “And although HIV can now be treated quite effectively, it can’t as yet be cured, so it can change people’s lives.”

“Poor Vivi,” Betty said with genuine sadness.

“It seems that Mike was worried that Linda had also been involved with Wayne,” Harry said carefully, realizing that she was treading on dangerous ground. Linda could very well deny having had an affair with Wayne to protect both herself and Mike. She wondered if Linda and Wayne had practiced safe sex and how long it would take Linda to realize that she’d better have an AIDS test.

“No!” Teresa exclaimed, sounding shocked.

“None of us can know for sure,” Harry said.

“Does Linda have AIDS? Is that why Mike killed Wayne?” Eddie asked.

Harry closed her eyes and recalled what Mike had said to her when they were in the water. “I don’t know what made him suspect that Linda had been unfaithful, but he thought Wayne might have given the virus to Linda, and perhaps she had passed it on to him. He also believed that Wayne was a man of no principles, and that he deserved to die.”

“No one has the right to play God,” Teresa said quietly.

“How very right you are,” Harry replied, looking Teresa in the eye.

“I don’t know about anybody else, but I’m ready for a good, stiff drink,” Betty said, lifting a brandy snifter from the rack. “Is anyone else interested?”

Predictably, everyone except Teresa was.

“I probably shouldn’t,” Harry hesitated.

“Don’t even think about it,” Judy warned.

“I’d like some water, then,” Harry asked. But Judy was prepared, and no sooner had she spoken than her lover placed a glass and an open bottle of mineral water on the end table.

“Actually, where is Vivi?” Dan asked.

“Gone,” Harry replied, pouring herself a glass of water and taking a sip. She explained what had happened on the beach

that evening. By the time she had finished, Dan had opened a
second bottle of brandy, and she was into her second bottle of
mineral water.

"God, I'm drunk," Eddie said, pouring himself another
inch of brandy. "And I think I deserve to be."

"I can't believe that Vivi is HIV positive," Betty said,
holding out her brandy snifter for Dan to fill. "I mean, is she
going to be okay?"

"She isn't sick yet. If she takes medication and looks
after herself, she might be okay for a long time," Harry said. She
rose slowly from the sofa and walked across the room to the
window. "Look at the fog. I can't even see the trees."

"Wayne's funeral is tomorrow," Betty said suddenly. "I
suppose everyone is planning to go."

No one answered, but Harry knew they would all be
there. Nasty, insensitive, irresponsible – he was still theirs.

"I'm going home," Eddie announced.

"Let's," Margaret agreed.

"Who's going to drive?" Harry asked. "In fact, who's
going to drive any of you? You're all too drunk to get behind the
wheel of a car."

"I drove you home last night, so you owe me one,"
Eddie said, dangling his car keys in front of Harry.

"Uh-uh, sorry, no way," Nora said. "Not with the
headache she's got."

"Teresa," he pounced.

"I don't have a driver's licence," Teresa replied.

"I guess we're going to have a good old-fashioned
slumber party," Harry commented. "It's probably just as well
with all this fog."

No one had much to say after that. Betty and Dan
wandered upstairs, then Margaret and Eddie and finally Teresa
and Nora. Some brandy snifters were abandoned on tables,
others on the floor, and nobody bothered to switch off the
overhead lights or the table lamps. Somehow Harry didn't think
that Mike or Linda would care.

"Judy," Harry said tentatively once they were alone in
the room.

"Yes," Judy replied, rising carefully from the bar stool.
There were tears running down her cheeks, which shocked
Harry.

"Let's go to bed," Harry said.

"Fine," Judy replied.

"I'm going to take a shower and wash off all this salt," Harry said through her exhaustion, as she cautiously crossed the living room and followed her lover into the downstairs bedroom.

"Fine," Judy said again.

Harry wanted to say something, but Judy had turned her back and was undressing. She trudged into the bathroom, stripped, and took a hot shower, carefully shampooing her hair and trying not to cry aloud when she touched the cut on her head. She dried herself and wrapped the towel around her body. Anything but that frilly bathrobe, she thought.

Judy was in bed when Harry returned to the room. After placing the towel on the back of a chair, she turned out the light and gingerly slid into bed. She felt Judy turn away from her.

"What's wrong?"

Her question was met with silence.

"Don't do this to me," Harry pleaded, placing her hand on Judy's shoulder. "I nearly died tonight."

"I'm so angry with you that I could kill you myself," Judy said bitterly.

"Can we talk about it?"

"How could you just fall into bed with a woman you knew was straight?" Judy railed, sitting up.

I should have known, Harry thought. She switched on the bedside table lamp and eased herself into a sitting position.

"Didn't you realize the risks you were taking? How could you do that to yourself? To us?"

"We practiced safer sex," Harry said softly. She had never seen Judy so infuriated or heard her sound so bitter.

"Really? What kind of safer sex? Casually safer, like it's one big joke or an opportunity to fool around with some kinky stuff? Semi-formally safer, with just enough latex to make you feel politically correct? Or the real thing?" Judy castigated her. "Can you tell me that you practiced one hundred per cent safer sex?"

"Yes," Harry said firmly, mentally thanking Vivi for having some sense in her head.

"What?" Judy said, looking astounded.

"We wore gloves the whole time, and there was no oral sex," Harry said. "She didn't even kiss me."

Judy slumped, closed her eyes, and began to sob.

"I'm sorry," Harry muttered as she put her arms around her lover.

Don't say that!"

"I know, you'll leave me if I apologize one more time," Harry said, gently rocking her from side to side.

Tears ran down Judy's cheeks and wet Harry's neck. "I was petrified that you hadn't taken any precautions. You were so close to being killed in the church, and then tonight you could have died if you'd lost your way in the fog or if Mike had caught you. And I don't know what I'd do without you, Harry, I really don't."

"And you won't have to find out," Harry responded quietly. "I'm here."

"When you said that Wayne had AIDS and that Vivi is HIV positive, I just couldn't stand it. I mean, I know that today, most people live a fairly normal life with HIV, but I freaked out. All I could think about what that eventually you were going to get sick and then you would wither away and die like to many of our friends did."

"I love you," Harry said. "I wouldn't ever do anything to threaten our relationship."

"Down deep, I know that," Judy replied. "But with everything that's gone on, I had a gut reaction."

Harry sent a silent thanks to Vivi, wherever she was, for having ensured that the sex they had engaged in was as safe as possible. Left to her own devices, Harry wouldn't have thought about it, even though she knew that Vivi was sexually active with men. "Nora thought the risk was really minimal, but she suggested that I have a test when I get back and then another in six months."

"I'm sure you're all right," Judy said.

"I am too," Harry replied. "But she said that we should take precautions."

"You mean…"

"Yes."

"For six whole months?" Judy cried.

Harry nodded.

Judy wiped a stray tear from her cheek as she stared at Harry and then said, "Oh, well. Maybe we can get dental dams at the wholesale price. Now turn that damn light out and let's get some sleep."

Harry switched off the lamp and snuggled up to Judy. It was Sunday night, and the reunion was over. Except for Harry and Teresa, everyone would be hung over in the morning. No one would want to talk. They would attend Wayne's funeral as a group, and then do their best to forget about what had happened. Wayne would not be missed, except perhaps by his family. And Vivi, who would likely both love and hate him for the rest of her life. The United Church would hire a new pastor, and eventually recover from the scandal of having had a murderer in its pulpit. Linda would likely put the cottage up for sale and leave Spruce Bay for parts unknown. And Vivi – well, Harry could only hope that she would get the medical care she needed and would one day read a newspaper or call someone and discover that she had not killed Wayne. No one deserved to go on thinking that she was responsible for taking another person's life.

"Harry?"

"Um?"

"Go to sleep," Judy mumbled.

"I was thinking about Vivi," Harry mumbled.

"I know," Judy sighed, turning around and giving her a hug. "But it's time to stop."

Judy was right. Tomorrow morning, they would drive to Halifax, fly home to Montreal, find the best deal they could on dental dams and then see if they could use them up in six months. And if she ever received another letter from one of her classmates about coming to Spruce Bay for a reunion, she was going to tear it up into tiny pieces and throw it in the garbage. With that comforting thought in her mind, she put her arm around Judy and fell asleep.

ABOUT THE AUTHOR

Thanks to my mother's artistic talents, I developed a passion for drawing and writing as a child. I started with simple drawings and gradually began writing longer captions, eventually transitioning to writing entire books. I wrote two books during my teenage years: a romance novel and a mystery involving an amateur detective and the perfume industry.

Growing up in a small town in Nova Scotia, I struggled with my sexual orientation and didn't have the right words to describe my feelings. It wasn't until later in life that I came out as a lesbian and met my wife. We recently celebrated our 50th anniversary in December 2022.

After a hiatus from writing, I began crafting short stories that were published in various publications. Early in my writing career, I published two collections of erotic short stories, which are now out of print.

I'm thrilled to collaborate with my new publisher, **Brainspired Publishing**, to revive my **Harriet Hubbley Mystery Series.**